My
Little Treasury
of
BEDTIME
STORIES

The Author

Nicola Baxter has written or
compiled over two hundred
children's titles. She has developed
ideas for a wide variety of international
publishers and particularly enjoys
the marriage of words and pictures
that children's books entail.
She lives in Norfolk, England,
with her little daughter.

The Illustrator

Jenny Press loves children's
picture books and fairy tales.
She has illustrated over fifty titles
and increasingly enjoys creating
the words as well as the pictures
of children's books. Jenny lives
in a small village in the east of
England with her dog Barney
and cat Jester.

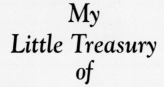

My
Little Treasury
of
BEDTIME
STORIES

Written by Nicola Baxter

Illustrated by Jenny Press

ARMADILLO

Published by Armadillo Books
an imprint of Bookmart Limited
Registered Number 2372865
Trading as Bookmart Limited
Desford Road, Enderby
Leicester, LE9 5AD, England

Reprinted 2001

ISBN 1-84322-030-X

Originally published as
5 Minute Bedtime Tales,
5 Minute Farmyard Tales,
5 Minute Kitten Tales,
and *5 Minute Teddy Bear Tales*

Produced for Bookmart Limited by Nicola Baxter
PO Box 215, Framingham Earl, Norwich NR14 7UR

Additional story ideas: Jenny Press
Editorial consultants: Ronne Randall, Jana Novotny Hunter
Designer: Amanda Hawkes

Printed in Singapore

Contents

Teddy Bear Tales

Farmyard Tales

Kitten Tales

Bedtime Tales

Teddy Bear Tales

Welcome to Bearborough!

Here are some of the fine and funny bears you will meet in this book.

Percival

Mother

Granny

Father

Bertram

Max

Barney

Cleo

Bedtime for Little Bears

All little bears love to snuggle down in their beds at night and go to sleep. But before they go to bed, little bears must have their baths, and some little bears just do not like to get their ears wet!

Once there was a little bear called Barney, who really hated his bath. His father tried everything to make bathtime fun. A huge boat and a bottle of the biggest bubbles you've ever seen didn't work. Three yellow ducks and some stuff that turned the water purple didn't either.

One day, Barney went for a walk with his granny. As they walked, it started to rain. Right away, Barney started to complain.

"I don't like getting wet," he whined. "It gets in my ears and in my eyes and up my nose, and it's horrible."

"Well, Barney, I am surprised," said Granny, "that you would want to give up all that good luck. Don't you know it's lucky for a little bear to get wet?"

The next night at bathtime, Barney's father was surprised to find that Barney jumped right into the tub with no fuss. And these days Barney is the luckiest bear you ever met—and the cleanest!

Big Bears, Little Bears

One day, Barney and his friend Cleo were playing in the park when some bigger bears came along.

"We're going to play on the swings, baby bears," they said rudely.

Barney frowned.

"We were here first," he said, "but we *could* go on the merry-go-round."

But as soon as Barney and Cleo were whizzing around, the bigger bears came along and wanted to play there, too. They weren't nice about it.

Cleo didn't want any trouble. "Let's go and play with our kite," she said.

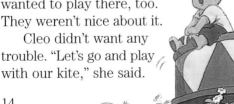

14

Soon the little bears were playing happily. But
before long, the big bears began to run around
playing ball. The park was plenty big enough for
everyone, but they insisted on
bumping into the little bears.

Just then, there was a huge gust of wind.
The big bears' ball blew under the caretaker's
cabin, and the little bears' kite flew into a tree.
Now none of the bears could play.

Barney was ready to start for home, but Cleo
had an idea. "You big bears are tall enough to
reach our kite," she said. "We are small enough
to crawl under the cabin and get your ball. What
do you think?"

The big bears looked ashamed. "We're sorry
we teased you," they said. "It's a good idea."

So everyone played happily together for
the rest of the day.

The Blue Bear

In a neat little house in the middle of Bearborough there lived a very silly bear. Albert always had to have the very latest things. He was so eager to keep up with fashion.

To be fair, Albert's clothes were sometimes wonderful, but more often he simply looked silly.

Each month, Albert's fashion magazines arrived in the mail. Usually they confirmed that he was the best dressed bear in town. On this particular morning, when he glanced at the covers, he gave a groan of despair. Blue! Everything must be blue! It seemed that nothing else would do at all.

Albert looked at his wardrobe with tears in his eyes. There were clothes of all kinds—but none were blue!

But that evening,
Albert had a great idea. What if
he could dye all his clothes? Then he
would be the height of fashion.

Albert had so many clothes, he
decided that only the ornamental pool in his
garden would be big enough to dye them in. He
tipped in pack after pack of dye. The water
became bright blue. Then he hurried to his
bedroom to begin carrying out the clothes.

Unfortunately, Albert tripped and
landed with a *splash!* in the pond.

Albert was dyed blue from ears to
paws. But did he learn his
lesson? No! He loved his new
blue fur. You won't find it
hard to spot him next time
you come to Bearborough!

The Bear on the Bus

Wednesday was market day in Bearborough. The bus was always full to bursting.

One Wednesday morning, Barney and his granny caught the bus into town. They had a lovely time. When it was time to come home, they once again squeezed onto the bus.

"It's standing room only," said Granny, "but I'll hold you up, Barney, so you can see out of the window."

But Barney soon found that the bear standing in front of him was much more interesting. He was an elderly bear, wearing a hat, and Barney was sure he had seen the hat move! There it was again! The hat gave a little jiggle, as though it was dancing.

The little bear wriggled with excitement.

"Granny," he whispered, "look!" Just then, the hat seemed to bounce. Granny gave a little scream. The bear in front turned.

"My dear lady," he cried, "let me introduce myself. I am Bertram Bear, and this," he went on, gallantly doffing his hat, "is my friend Percival."

Granny and Barney smiled when they saw the little mouse.

"I hope that we will all be the best of friends," said Bertram, smiling at Granny.

Teddy Bear Time

Visitors to Bearborough found it very confusing. You see, all the clocks in Bearborough were wrong. That was because old Mr. Minim the clock mender had become a little shaky on his legs. Although fit and well in every other way, he simply could not face climbing up a ladder to mend clocks high up.

As you can imagine, the trains were never on time, and the shopkeepers didn't know when to open their shops.

Then, one day, Bearborough had two very special visitors. They were a bear

called Alfred and his friend Jumble—who was an elephant! Now most bears in Bearborough had never seen an elephant before, so they all gathered round. And the elephant wrapped his trunk around each of the little bears in turn and lifted them up high, squealing with excitement.

"Excuse me, Jumble," said Mr. Minim. "Could you lift a grown-up bear like me?"

In seconds, Mr. Minim found himself dangling above the crowd, yet he felt as safe as if he was on firm ground.

And that is why, if you visit Bearborough these days, all the clocks are exactly right, for Jumble visits *every* year!

Uncle Hugo's Invention

Cleo's Uncle Hugo lived
in an old house on the edge of
Bearborough. Barney thought that
Uncle Hugo's house was the most
exciting he had ever been in. There was
a stuffed alligator in the hall and a real
live parrot in the living room. There were
collections of fossils and piles of books
everywhere. Uncle Hugo was an inventor.

At the moment, Uncle Hugo was inventing something new. It was the most extraordinary-looking machine.

"What exactly does it do?" asked Barney.

"It whistles," said Uncle Hugo. "I got the idea when the kettle boiled one day. I thought I could make a machine that would whistle in tune. Now for the moment of truth. I turn this switch here and the water in the boiler will start to steam. Prepare yourselves for a wonderful sound."

Soon there *was* a sound. It was the sound of Uncle Hugo zooming across the room on his machine and out into the garden.

"Hmm," said the old bear. "It's not, in fact, a whistling machine after all. It's a steam-driven mowing machine, and it works perfectly!"

The Snow Bear

When heavy snow fell in Bearborough, Cleo's little brother wanted to go out and play, but his mother said he must stay indoors.

"Don't worry, Max," said Cleo. "I'll build you a snow bear in front of the window."

No sooner had Cleo started piling up the snow, when Barney came past.

"Can I play too?" he asked. "I bet I'll build a better snow bear than you!"

"Just you come and try!" retorted his friend.

When some other little bears came along, Barney and Cleo told them about the snow bear competition, and they joined in.

Everyone was very busy—except Barney. He soon began throwing snowballs up into the trees. It was fun when the snow lying high up came down with a *whoosh!*

When the bears had finished, five fine snow bears stood in a row. Cleo's mother agreed to be judge.

"The one at the end is certainly the best," she said.

"It must be Barney's," said Cleo, "but where is he?"

Just then, Barney's bear collapsed in a heap—with Barney inside it!

"The snow from that tree fell on top of me," he laughed.

Follow the Rainbow

One Saturday morning, Barney went to the library for Story Time. Mr. Leaf the librarian read a story in which a pixie found a pot of gold at the end of a rainbow. It was very interesting, especially as it was raining!

When the children were ready to go home, the rain had stopped, but Barney didn't want to stop and splash in the puddles.

"Come on!" he said to Cleo. "We've got to hurry!" And he dragged the poor little bear along until they could both see that there was a beautiful rainbow in the sky.

"Quick!" cried Barney. "We've got to find the end!"

As they reached the top of the hill, they could clearly see the end of the rainbow. And it was in the middle of Barney's front garden!

Barney and Cleo flew down the hill, but as they reached the front gate, the rainbow disappeared!

Barney was still hopeful. "Maybe the pot of gold is still there," he said. "Where's my shovel?"

And before Cleo could stop him, he was busy digging up the tulip bed. Suddenly, something *clinked* on Barney's shovel and went flying toward his father, who had just appeared.

"It's the ring I lost last year!" he laughed, forgetting to be cross. "Maybe rainbows do have gold at the end of them!"

Mother Bear's Problem

One morning, Mother Bear had a worried look on her furry face. "I know there's something I'm supposed to remember about today," she said, "but I can't think what it is. I'm pretty sure it's something important."

"Never mind," said Mr. Bear at lunchtime. "If we have nothing else to do this afternoon, let's watch that old film on television. We can put our feet up and relax."

By half-past three, Mother Bear and her husband were settled on the sofa with mugs of coffee, a box of chocolates, and wearing their oldest, comfiest slippers.

The film was so exciting that Mother Bear almost forgot about her problem, until . . .

Driiiiing! . . . there came a ring at the doorbell.

Mother Bear felt a sinking feeling in her chocolate-filled tummy.

"Hello, darlings!" called Aunt Hortense, opening the door herself with a flourish. "I've come to stay as I promised!"

"I've remembered what I forgot," groaned Mother Bear to Mr. Bear, too softly for Aunt Hortense to hear. "I was going to suggest that we all went away for the weekend!"

How Many Paws?

Oone fine day, several little bears and their parents set off for a picnic at the beach. The grown-up bears carried huge baskets of goodies, while the little bears brought every pail and shovel they could find.

"Phew!" said Barney's father, when they reached the beach at last. "You little bears can start making sandcastles, while we get everything ready for lunch."

But it was such a wonderful, sunny day that almost all the grown-up bears had fallen fast asleep before the little bears had really started on their sandcastles.

"Look!" said naughty little Bettina, "while they are sleeping, we could taste the picnic."

One by one, the little bears squeezed their paws into a picnic basket and took a taste of the cake inside. It wasn't very long before all that was left of the cake was a pile of sticky crumbs.

"Oh dear," said Barney, when the grown-ups woke up, "I suppose it will be very hard to find out whether it was taken by seagulls or crabs or . . . turtles!"

"Or bears!" said his father. "I'm happy to say that it will be very easy to find out who has eaten the cake, because the chocolate has made lots of sand stick to their paws and noses!"

31

The Star Bears

L ate at night, when all his clocks were striking twelve, Mr. Minim the clock mender loved to sit at his bedroom window and look at the stars.

"I wish the young bears today were interested in astronomy," said Mr. Minim.

Next morning, Mrs. Bear and Barney came into Mr. Minim's shop. Mrs. Bear had brought her best clock to be mended.

"It used to keep good time," she said, "but last night it was almost midnight before Barney went up to bed because the clock was wrong."

"Almost midnight?" said Mr. Minim. "Then you must have seen the star bears."

"I did see the stars," said Barney, "but I didn't see any bears."

"That's because you didn't know where to look," said Mr. Minim. "I'll bring your clock back tonight at ten o'clock and show you."

That night, Mr. Minim showed the Bear family lots of interesting things. Best of all, he showed them the star bears.

"There's the Great Bear," he said, "and there's the Little Bear."

"Is he older than me?" asked Barney.

"Young bear," laughed Mr. Minim, "he's even older than me! And that really is old!"

33

The Lost Ribbon

In many ways, thought Cleo, Emmeline Bruin was the most annoying bear at school. All that Emmeline cared about was looking pretty. She wouldn't join in any rough games or play in the sand in case she got dirty. In fact, she was no fun at all.

One day, all the little bears went on a nature walk with their teacher, Mr. Tedson. They were told to collect fallen leaves.

"The shape of the leaf will tell you what kind of tree it has come from," said Mr. Tedson.

But the little bears had not been in the woods for long before Emmeline began to wail. "I've lost my best red ribbon!" she sobbed.

Cleo and the other bears began hunting for the ribbon.

In fact, it was Cleo who found it first. In a little bush beside the path, a tiny bird was busy weaving the ribbon into her nest.

Cleo could see at once that pulling out the ribbon would destroy the nest. Just then, Emmeline came up behind her. She was smiling. "Let's not say anything," she whispered. "It looks much prettier there than on my head!"

Cleo smiled back. You can't always tell what someone is like from the outside, she thought, looking at her new best friend.

Cousin Carlotta

One morning, Mrs. Bear got a letter. "It's an invitation," she said, "to a Grand Ball given by Mrs. Carlotta Carmody. I've never heard of her!"

Mrs. Bear turned the invitation over. Scribbled on the back was a short message.

"Dear Cousin, Yes, this is me, little Carly! I've married James Justin Jackson Carmody III. Do come to our party!"

"I don't believe it!" cried Mrs. Bear. "Cousin Carly was the scruffiest, untidiest, and, quite honestly, the messiest bear I ever knew. The very idea of that harum-scarum bear in a ball gown is quite beyond me. But we shall have to go, of course."

Three weeks later, the Bear family arrived at Cousin Carlotta's huge mansion.

"I feel faint," said Mrs. Bear. "Barney, there will be no running, no jumping, and definitely no sliding down stairs. All right?"

All the guests were waiting for their hostess to make her grand entrance.

"*Wheeeeeeeee!*" Cousin Carlotta made a grand entrance all right—sliding down the banisters!

Mrs. Bear forgot her nerves in a second. She ran forward to hug her cousin.

"Carly," she smiled, "you haven't changed a bit!"

The Bear on the Stairs

The Bear family enjoyed Cousin Carlotta's party enormously. "You must come back next week to see around the house," said Carlotta, as the Bears left.

The following Saturday, the Bear family arrived for lunch. Later, Mr. and Mrs. Bear set off for a Grand Tour.

Barney wandered around for a while, before going to sit on the staircase. He felt very bored and let out a big sigh.

"You could play with me, if you like," said a little bear on the stair above.

Barney jumped.

The bear was wearing strange clothes but he looked friendly. Pretty soon Barney and the bear, who said that his name was Charles, were playing a wonderful game.

"What have you been doing?" asked Barney's parents when they came back.

"I've been playing with Charles," said Barney, "but he seems to have disappeared."

"What did the little bear look like?" asked Carlotta, with a strange expression on her face.

Suddenly, Barney saw a picture of Charles on the wall.

"That's him," he said. "That's my friend Charles!"

Carlotta smiled. "That's my husband's great-great-great-grandfather," she said. "He lived over two hundred years ago—but he does like to make sure that young visitors feel at home!"

A Bear's Best Friend

One year, an uncle who lived overseas very unwisely gave Cleo a joke book for her birthday. It was dreadful. All day long, Cleo was trying out the jokes on her friends and family. And most of them were not very funny at all.

"What do you call a sleeping dinosaur?" she asked her father.

"I don't know, Cleo," groaned her dad. "What do you call a sleeping dinosaur?"

"A brontosnorus!" chortled Cleo. "What goes clomp, clomp, clomp, clomp, clomp, clomp, clomp, squoosh?"

"I'll make you go squoosh, if you're not careful," grunted her father. "I don't know. What does go clomp, clomp, etc?"

"An octopus with one shoe off!" Cleo couldn't stop giggling.

"Cleo! We didn't think they could get worse, but they

have!" cried her parents together. "How many more pages are there?"

"Oh, hundreds!" laughed Cleo, looking at her book. "Who is a bear's best friend?"

Cleo's father jumped out of his chair. "For once I know the punch line to that joke," he said. "A bear's best friend is the very sensible grown-up bear who takes away her joke book while some of her friends and family are still speaking to her!" He grabbed the book and took it away to his shed in the backyard.

Unfortunately, that was this morning, and Cleo's father has not been seen since, although the oddest sounds have been coming from the shed. They sound a lot like giggles!

The Striped Scarf

One afternoon, Mr. Bear came in for lunch rubbing his paws. "It's so cold," he said, "I thought my ears would fall off. What I need is a nice long red scarf." He knew that it was his birthday in a week's time.

Over the next few days, Barney noticed that his mother's workbag was bulging. He caught sight of some strands of red wool.

Mrs. Bear was on schedule until the day that Miss Bouquet in the flower shop complimented Mr. Bear on his blue sweater.

"You know," said Mr. Bear later, "I think if I were to have a scarf, it should probably be blue."

Mrs. Bear groaned. It was too late to start again. But Barney had a bright idea.

"What about stripes?" he suggested.

Well, that was a good idea, especially since, over the next few days, Mr. Minim commented on how much he liked Mr. Bear's yellow shirt, Mr. Leaf asked where he could get a green tie just like Mr. Bear's, and Barney, without thinking, asked if he could borrow his father's orange woolly hat.

On his birthday morning, Mr. Bear found the brightest and longest scarf you've ever seen.

"We're going to have to share this," he laughed. "It's long enough for the whole family!"

Paws With Patches

One day in a storybook, Cleo saw a picture of a bear with patches on his paws. Her mother explained that he was a bear who had done a lot of work with his paws, so they had worn out. A kind friend had sewn some patches on for him.

Cleo folded her arms and sat down.

"Aren't you going to help me put the book away?" asked her mother.

"No!" said Cleo.

Her mother could hardly believe her ears. Cleo was usually such a good little bear.

"Well, will you go and get your father?"
Cleo's mother tried again.

"No," Cleo said.

It was the same for the rest of that day.
Cleo wouldn't do anything.

"Sit down, Cleo," said her mother. "We
need to have a serious talk."

It wasn't very long before Cleo
explained. "I just don't want my paws to wear
out," she said, "so I'm saving them."

Cleo's mother laughed. "I'm surprised
about that," she said. "Most bears want
patches on their paws."

"Do they?"

"Oh yes, it's like wearing a medal. It
shows what a long and useful life you've led."

Well, ever since then, Cleo has been a
very helpful little bear, though her paws look
perfect to me!

The Singing Bear

At six o'clock in the morning, there is usually very little going on in Bearborough. That is why it was so shocking when the singing began.

TRA-la-la-la-la-la-la-LAAAAA!

It wasn't a horrible sound, but it wasn't the kind of thing you expect to hear at that hour of the morning.

The first time, bears shook their ears and thought they were dreaming. By the third morning, bears dressed in their nightclothes gathered in the street to try to stop the disturbance.

TRA-la-la-LAAAAA!

"It can't go on!" cried Mr. Minim, speaking for all of them.

"But listen!" Albert held up his paw. "It's beautiful, isn't it?"

And sure enough, it was.

Mr. Leaf the librarian put his head out of his front door. "It's my sister," he said. "She's an opera singer. Her stage name is Ursula Pallas. She's staying with me, and she has to rehearse."

Ursula Pallas? *The* Ursula Pallas? The bears were stunned.

"O-o-of course she must sing," stammered Mr. Minim. "She's the greatest singer in the world."

At that moment, a famous face appeared at the window.

"Darlings!" cried La Pallas. "I will perform especially for you, here in the square, tonight at seven."

The concert is still talked of in Bearborough. And they say that if you are very quiet, you can still hear the great Pallas's voice echoing softly around the square.

Bear Facts

Barney and Cleo were having supper at Barney's house. Cleo tried to entertain everyone by telling them interesting facts from her *Encyclopedia of Bears*.

Unfortunately, Mr. Bear liked to know best about everything, so he tried to think of something that Cleo might not know. But Cleo seemed to know everything!

In desperation, Mr Bear began to speak before he had really thought about what he was doing.

"The rarest bear of all," he said, "is the green bear of Thailand. It is almost never seen because it can hide so easily in the trees."

"A green bear? There isn't anything about it in my encyclopedia," said Cleo.

Mr. Bear felt that he had gone too far now to turn back.

"No," he said airily, "it is very, very rare. I was lucky enough to see one on my travels."

Mrs. Bear coughed loudly at the other end of the table.

"Your travels, darling?" she asked. "When was that? I feel I should warn you, Cleo, that there are bear facts and then there are bear-faced lies. You can't believe everything you hear."

"Oh, don't worry Mrs. Bear," said Cleo with dreadful honesty. "I don't believe everything that old bears say. Their brains go all mushy!"

The Flyaway Laundry

It was a beautiful windy day in Bearborough. Barney was helping his mother with the laundry. He carried the washing basket out to the clothesline and started to hang out the clothes. Oh dear, it wasn't easy! The wild wind tugged at the clothes before Barney could hang them out. And those clothes were really difficult to hold on to. First one of his father's socks went whirling away and over the fence. Then a T-shirt started flapping and flicking Barney on the nose. He held on as hard as he could, but still the T-shirt broke free and sailed away into the flower garden next door.

50

Just then, Barney's mother came out to see how he was doing.

"I'm sorry," gasped Barney, "but I just can't control this laundry!"

He had picked up one of his father's shirts, and it was struggling to get away.

"Hold on, Barney," cried his mother. "I'll hold on to the other sleeve!"

But as the two bears held on tight to the shirt, the wind puffed into it like a sail and lifted them both off their paws!

"Don't let go, Barney!" cried his mother, as they sailed over the fence.

"*Whee!*" called Barney. "This is better than flying my kite any day!"

The two bears landed with a bump in the field, still holding on to the shirt.

"I think it's too windy for laundry or kite-flying today," laughed Barney's mother, out of breath. "Let's have cocoa and cookies in front of the fire instead!"

Bears Ahoy!

Ever since their first meeting on the bus home from Bearborough, Barney's granny and Bertram Bear (and his friendly mouse) had been great friends. They liked to take young Barney out and about with them.

One day, Granny and Bertram arrived to take Barney on a mystery trip. As soon as he opened the door, Barney knew that he was in for an exciting day.

"Ahoy there, young bear!" called Granny and Bertram. They were dressed for a day on a boat.

"There she is, the *Ellie May*," said Bertram proudly, as they reached the bridge over the river.

Barney couldn't help feeling disappointed when he saw that the *Ellie May* was a very small boat! But Bertram's enthusiasm was catching.

"All aboard," he cried.

"Aye, aye, Captain," called Barney. "Can I be first mate?"

"I'm afraid that job's already taken," said Bertram, winking at Granny.

Instead, Bertram looked after the sandwiches. But when the Captain called for lunch, there didn't seem to be many left. Barney and Bertram exchanged a look of understanding.

"Pirates?" asked Bertram.

"Hundreds of 'em, Cap'n!" agreed Barney.

Are You There?

One wet afternoon, Cleo was very bored.

"Why don't you play with your brother?" asked her mother. "He's bored too."

Cleo looked cross. Max was too small to play the games she liked. Just then she saw him peek out at her between his paws. "Boo!" he said.

Cleo smiled. Maybe there *was* a game she could play with the baby. He put his paws over his face again. Cleo crept up close and whispered, "Are you there, baby bear?"

With a giggle, the little bear peeked between his paws.

"Es," he said and crawled away as fast as he could.

54

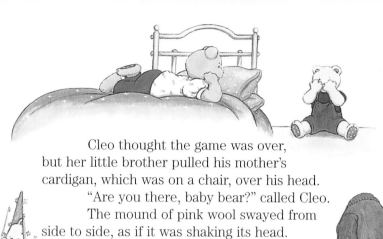

Cleo thought the game was over, but her little brother pulled his mother's cardigan, which was on a chair, over his head.

"Are you there, baby bear?" called Cleo.

The mound of pink wool swayed from side to side, as if it was shaking its head.

"Oh yes you are!" Cleo whisked the cardigan away, and her brother giggled again.

Pretty soon, the baby realized that he could hide behind things as well as under them. This time, Cleo hid her eyes as he crawled away.

"Are you there, baby bear?" she called.

Cleo had to hunt around the room to find that little bear. As she went, she called, "Where, oh where is baby bear?" and soon started making up rhymes to amuse him.

"Where, oh where is baby bear?
Is he here behind the chair?"

It was fun. When the little bears' mother came in, they didn't want to stop playing, and Cleo has loved her little brother even more from that day to this.

Mr. Bear the Baker

One morning, Barney's dad hurried him into the kitchen. "It's your mother's birthday tomorrow," he said, "and I thought we could bake her a cake."

The bears had a wonderful time, measuring, stirring, and mixing.

"I think that's about right," said Mr. Bear, looking suspiciously at the rather odd-looking mixture. "It's time to put it in the oven."

Pretty soon, there was a delicious smell coming from the oven. At least, there was after Mr. Bear remembered to turn it on.

"Time to clean up," he said. But somehow, both the bears got side-tracked. Mr. Bear felt that he must show off his egg-juggling routine. And Barney did a lot of useful

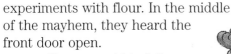

experiments with flour. In the middle of the mayhem, they heard the front door open.

Barney and his father rushed into the hallway, shutting the kitchen door behind them.

"You can't go in there for a minute," said Mr. Bear firmly to his wife. "We've been doing something extra secret."

Mrs. Bear looked at the two bears in front of her. "Not much of a secret when most of it is all over your fur," she said, "and if I pay attention to what my nose is telling me, I think it's time something extra secret came out of the oven."

It took Barney and his father the rest of the day to clean up the kitchen—but only ten minutes for them to help Mrs. Bear eat a strange-looking but completely delicious cake the next day!

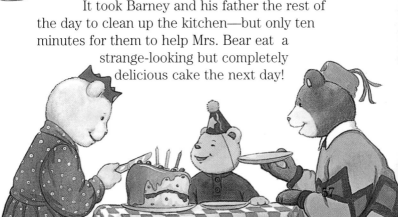

The Bravest Bear

One sunny afternoon, Cleo and Barney were drinking lemonade under a shady tree.

Cleo looked up at the branches.

"Are you afraid of heights, Barney?" she asked.

"Of course not," said Barney. "I can climb ever so high. I'll show you if you like."

And before Cleo could stop him, he was halfway up the tree.

"Come on up!" he called.

"No, no," said Cleo.

"You're not frightened, are you?" asked Barney.

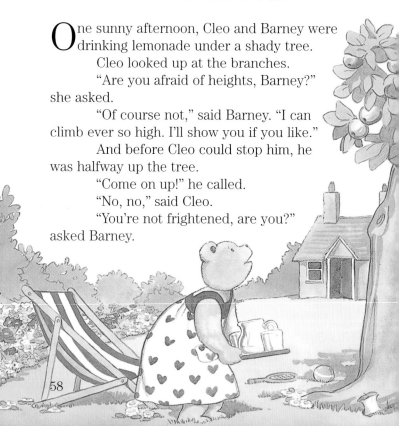

Barney made such a fuss that at last Cleo couldn't bear it any longer.

"All right!" she said. "Just watch me!" At first it was fine, but as soon as Cleo looked down, she began to shake.

"I don't like it, Barney," she said. "I really am afraid of heights."

"Scaredy-bear!" called Barney. "I'm much braver than you are! Ha ha!"

"I don't think so, Barney," said Mrs. Bear, who came out just then. "It took a lot of courage for Cleo to admit she was afraid."

Barney knew she was right and quickly helped his friend to the ground.

"Let's go and hunt for spiders," said Cleo. And Barney looked very worried indeed!

The Park Puzzle

One day, the whole Bear family decided to have a picnic in the park. After they had enjoyed the delicious food, all the grown-ups (and Bertram's mouse) fell asleep in the sun. Barney was very bored.

He tried tossing daisies into his father's hat, but one of them landed on Mr. Bear's nose.

Finally, Barney wandered off to explore. Behind some bushes near the tennis courts, he found a little cabin. Who could it belong to?

Barney walked back to his family. They were all still asleep, except for Bertram, who was decorating Granny's hat with daisies.

"You look worried," said Bertram.

"No," said Barney, "just wondering." And he told Bertram all about the little cabin.

"That will be the caretaker's cabin," said Bertram. "He's an old friend of mine, and I'm pretty sure I know what he'll be doing in there on an afternoon like this. Come with me."

Barney followed Bertram back to the cabin, and Bertram lifted him up to the window. Yes, there was the caretaker, doing just what Barney's family was doing back on the grass.

"I'll never understand grown-up bears," sighed Barney.

Please, Dad!

When Cleo and her family set off for a
weekend away, their little car was packed
to the roof with all the things that simply could
not be left behind. There was hardly any room
for the bears themselves!

Cleo's mother looked grim as she drove
down the lane, and her husband looked
desperate as he struggled to stop an enormous
map from flapping into her face. To be fair,
Cleo didn't help at all.

"Please, Dad," she said, after ten minutes,
"are we there yet?"

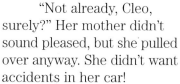

"We won't be there until very late at this rate," her mother replied. Mr. Bear was now so entangled with the map that he couldn't speak.

Cleo waited five minutes. "Please, Dad, can we stop?"

"Not already, Cleo, surely?" Her mother didn't sound pleased, but she pulled over anyway. She didn't want accidents in her car!

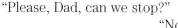

Cleo's Dad was flapping the map around in a worrying way.

"Please, Dad," Cleo began.

"If I hear one more word from you," said her mother grimly, "we'll go straight home. Is it right or left here?" Half an hour later…

"Please, Dad," said Cleo, "isn't that…?"

At the same moment they all realized they'd been going in a circle.

"Please, Dad," laughed Cleo. "I'm so glad to be home!"

Bertram's Books

One day, Bertram Bear decided to have a Grand Clear-out of his house. Barney and Granny agreed to help him, but they soon realized how big a job it was. There were books on every table and chair and piled up all over the floor.

"I just love books, you see," said Bernard.

"I quite understand, but why not donate them to the library after you have read them?" suggested Granny. "I'm sure Mr. Leaf would be very grateful."

"How clever you are, my dear, as always," said Bertram.

All afternoon, the bears carried books out to the front of the house, for the library van to pick them up later.

As Bertram and Granny sat down for a rest, they looked around for Barney. The little bear was nowhere to be seen.

After two hours of frantic searching, Granny was very worried indeed. But just then the van arrived from the library.

"Has anyone lost a small bear?" asked the driver, as he lifted some books from the huge pile. There was Barney!

He was hidden in a little house of books and enjoying an exciting storybook so much that he hadn't even noticed he had been walled in with books.

"I've heard of bookworms," laughed Bertram, "but it looks as though you and I are both book*bears*, young Barney!"

65

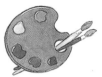

The Masterpiece

News soon spread around Bearborough that there was to be an Art Show. All bears had to do was send in their pictures. At the end of the show, the best grown-up picture and the best one by a little bear would receive a prize.

Of course, Barney, Cleo, and their families were all eager to enter the competition. Mr. Bear was particularly anxious to win.

"My work will be very modern," he said, "but I'm sure that is what the judges will be looking for."

On the day that the pictures had to be submitted, Cleo's mother agreed to take all of them, from both families, in her car. Each picture was framed and wrapped in brown paper, with a label giving the age of the painter. Painters' names were written on the backs of the pictures.

Cleo's mother lay the pictures carefully on the

back seat next to Cleo's baby brother's car seat. You can imagine how horrified she was when she arrived to find that the baby bear had spent the whole journey carefully pulling off the labels.

The harassed mother stuck them all back on as well as she could and carried them into the show.

On the last day of the show, everyone hurried to see what the judges had decided. Mrs. Bear looked at the pictures and smiled.

"Congratulations, sweetheart!" she told her husband. "You've won first prize!"

Mr. Bear's face lit up with pride, until his wife went on: "in the little bears' competition!"

Baby Bears

Barney didn't have any brothers and sisters, and he was sorry about that. When he saw Cleo playing with her baby brother, he thought what fun it must be.

"Couldn't we have a baby bear in our family?" he asked his mother one day.

Mr. Bear overheard Barney's question.

"One little bear is quite enough in this house," he laughed.

Still, Barney did think it might be better to be part of a bigger family. He decided to go and see Cleo to ask her what she thought.

But when Barney reached Cleo's house, the noise was incredible. "It's our turn to have the toddlers' group here," Cleo explained.

Barney looked down to find that one baby bear had dribbled on his paws, while another was busy trying to climb up his legs. Meanwhile, a third baby had climbed into a chair and a fourth was attacking a potted plant.

Barney hurried to rescue the baby in the chair and the potted plant.

"Thank you for coming along to help, Barney," said Cleo's mother. "It means that we grown-up bears can have a little rest."

It was Barney who needed a rest when he staggered home an hour later.

"Let's not have any more baby bears," he told his amused parents. "One little bear in this house is quite enough!"

A Bunch of Bears

Mrs. Bear gave Mr. Bear, who was reading his newspaper, a piece of her mind. "Granny and I have a lot to talk about and plan," she said. "Can't you and Bertram take Barney out?"

Bertram, who was settled in an armchair with an interesting book, looked up at the sound of his name. Barney, who was happily looking at a nature magazine on the floor, looked up too.

"Let's go," said Mr. Bear with a sigh. "Now what can a fine bunch of bears like us find to do on a sunny afternoon?"

The fine bunch of bears wandered off down the road. They watched half a game of tennis in the park. They played half a game of leapbear on the grass. Then they sat down for a rest.

"I'm exhausted already," said Barney's father. "What I really like to do on a day like this is sit down with my newspaper."

"And what I really like to do is read an exciting book," said Bertram Bear.

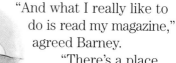

"And what I really like to do is read my magazine," agreed Barney.

"There's a place where we can do all that," said Bertram. The fine bunch of bears spent a lovely afternoon doing what they liked best—in the library! "It's nice to have a change!" laughed Mr. Bear.

A Perfect Party

Bertram Bear was beside himself with excitement. He was going to give a party. All his friends in Bearborough—and that was a lot of bears!—would be invited.

So Bertram got busy. He spent hours in the kitchen, making all the things that bears love to eat—especially granny bears. As the day of the party drew near, he even made a big effort with the cleaning and filled his rooms with flowers and balloons.

On the day of the party, when he was sure that everything was perfect, he put on his best suit and sat down to wait for his guests to arrive. He waited and waited. The minutes passed . . . and passed . . . but no one came. Bertram's head drooped. He fell asleep.

Driiiiing! Bertram's doorbell woke him. He leaped forward in excitement, but realized as he did so that it was already getting dark—much too late for party guests.

On the doorstep stood Granny. "I know what you said, my dear," she smiled, "but I wondered if you wanted any help for tomorrow."

"Tomorrow?" replied Bertram faintly. Then he opened the door wide and began to laugh.

Next day, every single bear that Bertram had invited hurried over to Bertram's house for his party. This time, Granny did help him to get the food ready—again. She didn't tell a soul, but she shared several secret smiles with Bertram during the evening. And the party? It was perfect!

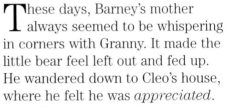

Poor Bear!

These days, Barney's mother always seemed to be whispering in corners with Granny. It made the little bear feel left out and fed up. He wandered down to Cleo's house, where he felt he was *appreciated*.

But Cleo told him she was too busy to play.

"I'm helping to look after my brother," she said. "He's not very well, poor bear!"

Barney looked so forlorn for a moment, that Cleo's mother asked him to come in anyway. "There's some ice cream left over from the invalid," she said.

Barney sat and ate ice cream and watched Cleo and her mother getting nice things for the sick little bear. Suddenly he had an idea.

Next day, Barney put his plan into action. "I'm not feeling well," he told his mother, who was talking to Granny on the phone.

"Ssssh! I can't hear," said Mrs. Bear.

"I'm not well," moaned Barney.

Mrs. Bear put down the phone and placed one paw on Barney's forehead.

"It's nothing serious," she said. "Where does it hurt exactly?"

"All over," mumbled Barney.

"This isn't like you, Barney." said Mrs. Bear. "Poor bear! I wonder if it might be because I haven't had much time recently to talk to my best little bear? How would it be if I told you a Very Big Secret?" And she whispered in his furry ear.

"Now, are you still feeling ill?"

"Me? Never!" said the little bear.

Martha Makes a Wish

One morning, Barney took breakfast in bed to Granny. "I thought I should have a practice," Barney told Granny, "before next week."

"Why?" teased Granny. "What's happening next week?"

"But I thought you knew!" cried Barney, his eyes open wide. "You're going to marry Bertram!"

"So I am," laughed Granny. "So you're going to bring me breakfast in bed on my wedding day, are you?"

"Yes," said Barney, "and every day after that."

"But Barney," said Granny gently, "hasn't anyone told you? After that, I'll be living at Bertram's house."

Barney's face fell. He hadn't thought about that at all. He really liked Granny living at home.

"I wish you could stay here," he said. "I wish you weren't getting married at all!"

Granny cuddled the little bear. "I'm going to tell you a story," she said, "about a bear called Martha. When she was young, she met and married a wonderful gentleman bear called Edward. They were very happy. Then, just as they were looking forward to a peaceful time together, Edward died and left Martha all alone. She thought she would never be happy again, although she had a dear little grandson. She wished for the sun to shine for her again. And one day, Martha met a funny bear with a mouse in his hat. She felt so lucky to have a second chance to be happy. Now do you understand, honey?"

"Yes," smiled Barney, "I do."

Granny Bear's Boots

There are a lot of things to be organized before a wedding, but Granny and Barney's mother managed to sort everything out. Then, one evening at supper, Granny suddenly said, "What if it rains?"

"We can have everything inside," said Mrs. Bear calmly. "There's no problem at all."

"Oh yes there is," declared Granny Bear. "I still have to get out of the car. What if there are puddles for my beautiful new shoes? What if it rains on my wonderful wedding hat?"

"My dear," smiled Mr. Bear, "I will personally go into town and buy you the loveliest umbrella I can find. But I really don't know what to do about your shoes."

Of course, Barney had been listening.

"What she needs is a good pair of boots," he told Cleo, "but I don't think you can get special waterproof wedding boots."

"I know!" cried Cleo. "We can decorate her ordinary boots. It will be fun. Come on!"

Cleo found paints, paper, sequins, and even some ribbons, while Barney crept off to "borrow" the boots. He and Cleo had a lovely time decorating the boots with everything they could find.

That evening, Bertram came by to take Granny for a walk by the river. The ground was a little damp, so Granny hurried off to put on her boots—and came back roaring with laughter.

"It was a lovely idea, Barney," she said. "But what will people think if I wear them now?"

"Sweetheart, they will think you look beautiful," said Bertram. "And as for the wedding, you don't need to worry at all. Naturally, the groom will carry the bride —like this!" And to Barney's amazement, the sprightly old bear scooped up Granny and carried her off—boots and all!

The Bouncing Bear

Cleo and Barney were playing in the park. "I love swinging," said Cleo. "You can see all sorts of things that you can't see from the ground."

"Yes," said Barney, as he swung past, "like trees and bushes and bouncing bears. Yes, look, a bouncing bear!" It was true. Every few seconds, the smiling face of a bear appeared above the bushes opposite.

"I recognize that bear," said Barney. "It's Bingo from school. He's younger than us, Cleo, but look how high he's jumping! I thought I was the best jumper!"

"You are, Barney," said Cleo loyally, but she had to admit that even Barney couldn't possibly jump so high.

"We should say hello anyway," said Cleo firmly. "Come on." But as they walked around the bushes, Cleo and Barney started laughing. Bingo had a trampoline!

"Come and try it!" shouted the little bear.

Recently, Mrs. Bear has wondered why her bed springs seem to have lost their spring. I think I can guess. Can you?

Ready, Set, Go!

School sports day arrived at last, and Barney was determined to do his best. All too soon, Mr. Tedson was blowing his whistle for the first race. "All bears to the starting line! Ready, set, go!"

Barney ran as fast as he could, but just as he reached the finish line, Cleo came sailing past and won the race.

It just wasn't Barney's afternoon. For one reason or another, he finished second in everything he tried. He slipped on the grass in the high jump. His shorts fell down in the hopping race! In the egg-and-spoon race he ran the wrong way!

82

By the time the last race was called, Barney had given up. And to make matters worse, as all the little bears got ready on the starting line, a large butterfly came and landed on Barney's nose.

Barney didn't want to hurt it, so he concentrated very hard and blew ever so gently. The butterfly fluttered safely away, just as Mr. Tedson was saying, "…set, go!"

Maybe it was because the butterfly had calmed his nerves, but Barney ran the race of his life. He sailed over the finish line in front of all the other bears.

"Barney! Barney!" came a loud chant from the crowd, but Barney was so happy to have won that even his dad couldn't embarrass him as he held his winning cup.

The Very Best Bear

Granny Bear need not have worried. When Barney brought her breakfast in bed on her wedding morning, the sun was shining and there wasn't a cloud in the sky.

Much to Mrs. Bear's amazement, everything was right on schedule. But just as the Bear family was leaving the house, the telephone rang.

"Don't worry, we'll think of something," the others heard her say, as she put the phone down.

In the car, Mrs. Bear explained that Bertram's best bear's car had broken down, and he wouldn't be able to make it in time.

"What's a best bear?" asked Barney.

"It's a special friend of the bridegroom," explained his father. "My best bear was Uncle George."

Bertram was waiting on the steps, as the Bear family arrived. He didn't look worried at all.

"You seem to have solved your problem," said Mr. Bear.

"I have now," said Bertram. "I've decided to ask the bear who brought Martha and me together to be our best bear. Come on, Barney, it's time to go!"

So Granny's happiest day was Barney's proudest day, too, and most of their friends from Bearborough were there to make sure that it certainly was a day to remember.

Farmyard Tales

Welcome to Windytop Farm!

There's always something happening down on the farm when these friends get together!

Farmer Barnes Annie Harold

Duchess

Pompom

Delilah

Cackle

Lala Lamb

Biggy Pig

Busy Hen

Denby Dog Pup Dymphna Mrs. Speckles

Sweet Dreams, Harold!

When you have a warm, dry stable, filled with fresh, golden straw, and your tummy is full of oats and carrots and other good things, you should be able to get a good night's sleep—if you're a horse, of course! But poor old Harold Horse spent all day dozing in the sun.

"It's because I can't get a wink of sleep at night," he told Busy Hen.

"It's those mice. Am I right, Harold?" asked Busy. "For you have a fine stable, much nicer than our old henhouse."

"Quite right," agreed the old horse. "They are scritch-scratching all night long. I can ignore the wind blowing and the rain falling. But I can't ignore this."

"Leave it to me," said Busy Hen.

Later in the day she went to Harold's stable and had a very long conversation with a little person with a twitchety nose and a long tail.

A week later, Harold was trotting about the farmyard as usual, much to everyone's great delight.

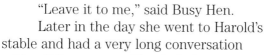

And Busy Hen was as proud as punch of the brand new henhouse that Farmer Barnes had built for all the hens.

"I knew Farmer Barnes wouldn't leave us in that old henhouse once it had mice in it," she clucked. "And those mice just love their new home—so everyone's happy!"

The Cluckety Duck

Farmer Barnes' duckpond was never a very peaceful place. Those ducks were always making a noise.

One day, Farmer Barnes brought a new duck to the pond.

"Be nice to her, you daffy ducks," he said. "She's not used to your quacky, splashy ways."

For several days, the little duck paddled shyly around the pond and didn't say a word.

At last Dymphna, who was curious about the newcomer, waddled up and asked her how she liked her new home. The duck looked up and opened her beak. She said her first word on Windytop Farm. It was … "Cluck!"

Dymphna was so surprised. Whoever heard of a clucking duck? And the trouble was that none of the ducks could understand a word she clucked.

Dymphna consulted Busy Hen, who knew several foreign languages, and Busy Hen talked to the newcomer.

"It's quite simple," she told Dymphna that evening. "This little duck is an orphan. She was brought up by an old lady's French hen. So of course, she has never learned to speak duck language. We will have to teach her."

The new duck, whose name was Dolores, was a very quick pupil. How proud of her Dymphna and Busy Hen were when she dived into the pond with a loud, "QUACK!"

I'm afraid the duckpond is noiser than ever these days!

Biggy Pig's Problem

Biggy Pig was the oldest pig on Windytop Farm and he was also the biggest. That, of course, was how he got his nickname.

One day, Farmer Barnes leaned over Biggy Pig's sty and scratched his back with a stick.

"Old friend," he said, "there's a very important day coming up for you on Friday. I want you to eat as much as you can, so that you're as big and fat as can be."

Biggy gulped. "I'm very much afraid," he told Harold later, "that Farmer Barnes means to take me to the market on Friday."

Harold looked serious. "That's terrible, Biggy," he said.

94

"There's only one thing you can do. Diet! No one takes a thin pig to market."

So for the next few days, Biggy hardly touched his food.

But when Friday came, Farmer Barnes didn't take Biggy to the market at all. He took him to the County Show. You should have seen how proud he looked as he arrived back at the farm—with his First Prize ribbon!

Where's That Goat?

Scraggles the goat was not popular with the other animals. You just couldn't trust Scraggles. To a goat, almost everything looks like food. In fact, almost everything *is* food.

One day he ate Harold's best bridle. The old horse was really upset.

"Isn't there something we can do to stop that wretched goat?" asked Busy Hen, who had lost several nests of straw.

"No, my dear," crowed Cackle the rooster. "I'm afraid goats will be goats." And that really was the wisest thing that Cackle, who was not known for his brains, had ever said.

But as things turned out, the animals didn't have to do anything. Scraggles did it all by himself. One breezy morning, when the sun was shining, he took a liking to Farmer Barnes' laundry, flapping in the wind. He munched through three pairs of socks, half a shirt, the bottom of a nightshirt, and several pairs of underwear.

Just then, Farmer Barnes came back for his lunch. He went straight to his workshop to find a stout chain and an even stouter stake. Now Scraggles has to content himself with a fresh patch of grass every day and no socks at all!

Busy Hen's Chicks

One spring day, Busy Hen sat down on her nest and stayed there.

Of course, all the animals knew what *that* meant. Busy Hen was going to hatch out some baby chicks.

"How many will it be this time, Busy Hen?" called Harold the horse as he clip-clopped by on his way to the meadow.

Busy Hen began counting. "Er … ten and then some more," she said at last. Hens are not very good at counting, although they are excellent with foreign languages.

Even for Busy Hen, that was a lot of eggs,
but she sat and she sat until all thirteen fluffy
chicks were hatched. She didn't sleep a wink
that night, as she guarded her precious babies.

But next morning, the little
chicks became restless. First one
and then another wobbled off on
spindly legs to explore.

"Help!" called Busy Hen.
She didn't know what to do.
Thirteen chicks were just too
many. She couldn't run in thirteen
directions at once.

It wasn't until Biggy Pig suggested
a babysitting service that Busy Hen heaved a
sigh of relief. Each little chick found itself with
an extra special aunt or uncle.

"I like being an uncle!" puffed
Harold Horse, "but it's hard work!"

Little Lala Lamb

When the snow was lying thick on the ground at Windytop Farm, Farmer Barnes set off to find his sheep.

The snow had come just when he was expecting the sheep to start having their lambs, and he was afraid the little ones would not survive the bitter cold.

You can imagine how relieved he was to find the sheep sheltering behind a wall. And none of them had yet had their lambs.

But when the sheep were in the barn, he counted them to make sure they were all there. They weren't. One sheep was missing.

Farmer Barnes went out into the cold again. Out on the hill once more, he searched everywhere. At last, he heard a little sound. It sounded like someone singing, right by his feet!

Farmer Barnes bent down and began to dig with his bare hands. Just below the surface he came upon two bright little eyes—and then two more! The missing sheep had had her lamb, and it was the little lamb who was singing, buried in the snow.

"I'm going to call you Lala," Farmer Barnes told her. "Because if you hadn't sung your lala song, you and your mother might never have come safely home."

Farmer Barnes' Apple Pie

One summer, Farmer Barnes bought a pair of geese. They were beautiful white birds who honked when anyone came near them.

"There have been a lot of burglaries around here," the farmer told them. "Your job is to warn me if any strangers come to Windytop Farm. In return, you can run about in my lovely orchard all day long."

The very next day, when the farmer was away cutting barley, two men drove into the farmyard in an old truck. They checked that no one was about, then they hurried over to the pigsty and started scooping up the piglets.

The piglets squealed, but that was nothing to the noise the geese made in the nearby orchard. They honked and spread their

wings. And they ran
so quickly towards the
rickety fence that they broke
right through it and came
rushing into the farmyard,
where the men were just
loading the last little piglet
into the back of their truck.

But at the sight of the
geese, the men ran for their lives,
leaving the piglets behind.

Farmer Barnes was very, very pleased. But when
autumn came, and the orchard was full
of beautiful apples, those
geese wouldn't let him in!
Farmer Barnes was a fair
man. "Okay," he said, "you
deserve some rosy apples,
and I can go without my
apple pie—this time!"

103

Duchess and Delilah

When the farm animals saw Duchess the cow with a pretty young calf by her side one morning, they were surprised.

"I didn't know she was expecting a baby!" hissed Dymphna to the other ducks.

Even more strange was the way Duchess treated her calf. She was very off-hoof about the whole thing. At last the story to come out. The calf came from a nearby farm.

"Duchess," Farmer Barnes had said to his most motherly cow, "this little calf's mamma can't look after her, so I want you to do it. You'll take care of her so well."

Duchess did try to be kind to the calf. She made sure she had

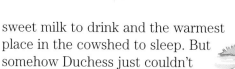

sweet milk to drink and the warmest place in the cowshed to sleep. But somehow Duchess just couldn't warm to her new daughter.

"I can't forget that she isn't really my own calf," she told Busy Hen. "And she's called Delilah. Such a silly name!"

The little calf turned out to be very adventurous. One day, she got into real trouble. There was a commotion from the duck pond and a frightened cry from the calf. She had fallen into the water, but she hadn't learned to swim!

While all the animals were wondering what to do, Duchess strode into the pond, grabbed the little calf by her tail, and hauled her out of the water.

She was beaming as she licked the calf's face dry. "I did what any mother would do," she said. "You know, Delilah is such a pretty name."

A Stitch in Time

Busy Hen was not usually afraid to speak her mind, but there were some subjects that even she felt were a little delicate. She confided in her friend, Mrs. Speckles.

"Surely someone else has noticed?" she clucked. "I don't like to say anything, but really something should be done."

"Aaah," said Mrs. Speckles wisely. She knew exactly what Busy Hen was talking about. Earlier in the week, Farmer Barnes had torn the seat of his trousers on some brambles, and ever since, although he seemed not to notice, you could see a large portion of his underwear!

"I can guess what you're thinking," she went on. "If you and I and some of the other ladies paid Farmer Barnes a little visit one night…?"

"How about tonight?" agreed Busy Hen.

And that is why, late that night, while the farmer snored in his bed, Busy Hen and some of her friends hopped in through the window and got to work with needles, thread, and a piece of Harold's oldest blanket.

Next day, Farmer Barnes appeared in his patched trousers in all their glory.

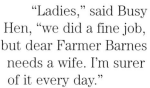

"Ladies," said Busy Hen, "we did a fine job, but dear Farmer Barnes needs a wife. I'm surer of it every day."

The other hens agreed, and when Busy Hen makes up her mind about something, it is almost sure to happen!

Harold Saves the Day

Some of the smaller animals were covering their ears on Windytop Farm. Farmer Barnes was red in the face and shouting—and some of his language really wasn't fit for little ears to hear.

Everyone knew their dear old farmer wasn't really furious with his old tractor. He was just annoyed that the tractor wouldn't start.

"He has that brand new shiny one," crowed Cackle to Biggy Pig. "Why can't he use that?"

Biggy Pig sighed. "Because, Cackle," he said, "the old tractor is standing in front of the barn so the new tractor can't get out."

"Can't he push it out of the way?" asked Cackle.

"You try," suggested Biggy Pig. And I'm afraid that Cackle really has no brains at all, because he did!

Poor Farmer Barnes looked hopelessly at the tractor. Just then, he heard a friendly clip-clopping noise. It was Harold. The farmer looked up as the old horse nuzzled the top of his head with his nose. All at once, a smile came over the farmer's face.

"Harold!" he cried. "How do you feel like some work? Like in the old days?" The farmer harnessed Harold to the old tractor. Then the old horse began to pull. Cackle was so impressed that he fell off his perch. And as the tractor rolled out of the way, *everyone* cheered.

The Paint Problem

One fine, still day, Farmer Barnes decided to give the doors and windows of the farmhouse a new lick of paint.

But Farmer Barnes was not a man who enjoyed spending money. "Waste not, want not," was his motto. He went into his old workshop and rummaged about until he found eleven—yes, eleven—cans of old paint. There was some red, some orange, a brilliant turquoise, white, a lot of green, some black, a tiny bit of silver, a pale yellow, two tins of dark brown, and a very vivid violet.

"He can't really be thinking of using all of them," hissed Biggy Pig to Cackle. "It's going to look awful!"

It was just at this moment that Annie, who came to collect the eggs, drove into the farmyard.

110

She was a comfortable-looking lady with clothes that looked almost as old as Farmer Barnes'. "Afternoon, Fred," she called. "What are you doing?" Farmer Barnes explained.

Now even Annie could see that it was not a good idea to paint a house using ten different paints. She told Farmer Barnes exactly what she thought. And she told him straight. Farmer Barnes felt pretty foolish. Still … the paint was too good to waste.

Farmer Barnes fetched one of Biggy's old water troughs and poured every drop of paint into it. Then he stirred it with a big stick. Now the paint was all the same—a muddy shade of brown.

When the house was painted, it looked terrible. But Dymphna sighed a sigh of pure happiness. "Beautiful," she said. "As I always say, you can't beat mud, can you?"

Windy Windytop

There's a reason why Windytop Farm is called Windytop Farm. It is on top of a hill, for one thing, and it's very, very windy for another.

One windy day, when Cackle had been blown off his perch on the henhouse roof for the fourth time, Duchess the cow called the animals together.

"This wind is getting worse," she said. "I can't remember it being as bad as this when I was young. I put it down to the windmills."

"What windmills?" asked Biggy Pig. "There are no windmills."

"Exactly!" cried Duchess eagerly. "In the old days there were windmills to use up the wind. Now it can just blow free."

Biggy Pig felt that the conversation was getting out of hand. "Never mind why there's more wind," he said, "we've got to find a way of dealing with it."

Just then one of Farmer Barnes' sheets, which he had put on the line to dry in the wind, flapped past. It had escaped!

Without thinking what he was doing, Biggy Pig grabbed the passing sheet with two trotters—and took off! The world's first hang-gliding pig sailed over the farm.

Busy Hen covered her eyes with her wings. But whether Biggy Pig was using up the wind, or whether it just dropped of its own accord, the day was suddenly very still. Biggy Pig had had a wonderful time, even if he hadn't planned on a water landing!

Mrs. Marchant's Visit

Farmer Barnes didn't have many visitors. So when he started tidying up the yard one day, the animals got very excited.

"Someone's coming, mark my words," said Busy Hen.

"Maybe he's found a wife," said Dymphna, hopefully.

"But he hasn't met anyone," replied Busy Hen.

The animals didn't have long to wait for the visitor. Two days later, a shiny car swept into the yard. A lady got out and walked delicately across the yard on her high heels.

Before the lady even reached the farmhouse, Farmer Barnes came out. He was wearing his old suit.

"Mr. Barnes, how do you do?" said the lady. "Will you show me around?"

"Mrs. Marchant? Please come right this way," replied the farmer.

"He likes her," squealed Dymphna. "She's going to be Mrs. Barnes!"

"Be quiet, Dymphna!" whispered Busy Hen. "She's here for business. Anyone can see that."

"I think we can agree your loan," said Mrs. Marchant later, as she climbed back into her car.

Dymphna reported to the other animals. "She's not going to marry him," she said sadly. "She said, 'I think we can agree you're alone.'"

Busy Hen sighed. She would have to explain to the other animals later that Farmer Barnes' loan for the new barn was his only business with Mrs. Marchant.

Little Pig Gets Lost

Although there were lots of piglets on Windytop Farm, one in particular caught Farmer Barnes' eye. Like his great-uncle Biggy Pig, he had all the signs of being a champion, and Farmer Barnes did like to win ribbons at the County Show. He called the piglet Little Pig. Of course, like Biggy, Little Pig had a long, grand name as well, but no one could ever remember what it was.

Farmer Barnes wanted Little Pig to grow big, but Little Pig surprised everyone by wanting to do sports!

116

He liked to go for a run every morning and to find lots of time for jumping and diving practice. "He'll never put weight on at this rate," said Biggy Pig, shaking his head.

Then, one day, Little Pig went missing.

"He's only a little pig," said Biggy. "We need to search the farm."

But an hour later, the animals gathered under the old oak tree without Little Pig. They were now very worried indeed. It was just then that Biggy's sharp ears heard a little squealing sound.

Hardly able to believe their eyes, the animals looked up, and up, and up … right to the top of the tree. A little pink face looked down at them. "I was climbing," said Little Pig, "but I got stuck!"

Busy Hen soon flew up and guided Little Pig down. He was very grateful. You know, after that, Little Pig wasn't quite so keen to test his sporting abilities!

Cackle Crows Again

One morning, the sun was already high in the sky when Farmer Barnes came stomping out of the farmhouse.

"I don't know what's the matter with me," he muttered. "I don't think I've ever woken up late before."

The first thing Farmer Barnes did every morning was to milk Duchess the cow. He expected to see her waiting at the gate, but Duchess was fast asleep under a tree, with Delilah next to her.

It was the same when Farmer Barnes went to feed Biggy Pig. The farmer found

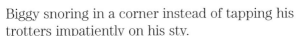

Biggy snoring in a corner instead of tapping his trotters impatiently on his sty.

Farmer Barnes soon found that all the other animals were sleeping peacefully. Then, all of a sudden, he realized what the problem was. Every creature on the farm was awakened each morning by Cackle the rooster, crowing at the top of his voice. This morning, Cackle hadn't crowed!

When Farmer Barnes finally found Cackle hiding in a corner of the barn, he couldn't help laughing. As usual, Cackle had been poking his beak into places he shouldn't. This time it was a bucket of tar. Now he couldn't open his beak to cackle, crow or peck.

Farmer Barnes soon cleaned him up. And for a whole week, neither Farmer Barnes nor the rest of the animals grumbled when Cackle began to crow at the crack of dawn—even when he gave them extra-early double crowing!

Mrs. Speckles and the Cat

When Mrs. Speckles is upset about something, *everyone* knows it. One morning, Mrs. Speckles was more upset than usual.

"It's that cat!" she cried. "She's sitting on the henhouse roof and she's been there all night! It's not as if she really lives here!"

It was true. The fat, fluffy cat who spent all her time on the farm really belonged to an old lady down the road. Each morning, the old lady brushed Pompom, as she called her cat, and tied a beautiful bow around her neck. The old lady had no idea that her cat spent every day on Windytop Farm.

Just then, Farmer Barnes came out of the farmhouse. When he spotted Pompom he came right over and picked her up.

"I thought you might be here," he said. "Your mistress had to move to a special home, where she can be looked after properly. She has asked me if I will look after you. But I'm afraid this will have to go. You're a farm cat now." And he gently pulled Pompom's bow from around her neck.

Just then, one of the little mice who lived in the old henhouse took advantage of the commotion to have a look around in the new henhouse. The hens spotted him with horror. But so did someone else. In a flash, Pompom dashed into the henhouse and chased the mouse out.

As the cat strolled back, Mrs. Speckles spoke. "Welcome to Windytop Farm!" she said.

The Trouble With Denby Dog

Farmer Barnes took good care of all his animals, but Denby Dog was special. He had worked with the farmer for more years than either of them could remember.

But Denby Dog was getting old. Farmer Barnes became worried about him.

"Old fellow," he said, "the wind is bitter this morning. Why not stay beside the fire?"

But the old dog gave Farmer Barnes such a mournful look that he couldn't bear to leave him behind. Later, Denby explained to Biggy Pig how he felt.

"I've been with Farmer Barnes for years," he said. "What if something happened to him away in the fields and I wasn't there to run for help? No, I must do my job."

Strangely enough, it was also to Biggy Pig that Farmer Barnes explained his worries. "Old Denby simply isn't up to the job any more. I've bought a new pup. He'll be arriving tomorrow, but I hate to hurt the old boy's feelings."

Biggy Pig snorted. He felt sure everything would be fine. And it was.

When the puppy arrived, Denby Dog got straight down to business. "It's high time I retired, young pup," he said. "And now that there'll be someone to follow in my pawprints, I can do it at last. But first, there's a lot I've got to teach you. Follow me, and leave those chickens alone!"

Dymphna to the Rescue

At very busy times on the farm, Farmer Barnes asked his old friend Annie to come each day to take care of the animals.

Now Annie was not the most efficient person. She was likely to forget things and drop things, but Annie was very fond of the animals, and anyone can forgive a knocked-over grain bucket or a late lunch for that.

One morning Farmer Barnes left Annie in charge. "The mechanic is coming to have a look at my old tractor this morning," he said. "Here are the keys. They're the only set I've got, so please don't lose them."

Annie put the keys in her pocket. Then she set off to fetch Biggy Pig's breakfast. But on the way she stopped to help a little duckling back to the pond. As she did so,

124

there was a loud splash. The tractor keys had fallen out of her pocket and into the water!

Busy Hen—as usual—had seen everything that happened. She at once hurried off to find Biggy Pig.

"You like wallowing about in mud, Biggy," she cried. "Can't you find those keys for Annie?"

"My diving days are over," sighed Biggy. "Mud is one thing, but water is quite another."

Busy Hen had run out of ideas, when Dymphna Duck strolled up. "Is this what you're looking for?" she asked, dropping the keys at Annie's feet.

Annie was so grateful to Dymphna that she gave her the ham and mustard sandwiches from her lunchbox. And Dymphna kindly shared them with Busy Hen —although the fact that she hated mustard might have had a little to do with it too!

Farmer Barnes' Spring Clean

Farmer Barnes does like things to be clean, and on a busy farm that's pretty difficult. So that is why, once a year, Farmer Barnes has his big Spring Clean. Everything gets cleaned, from the cupboard under the sink to the roof of Biggy Pig's sty.

You've never seen so much washing and brushing, dusting and polishing. All the animals join in.

The last stage of the Spring Clean takes place in the farmhouse. Farmer Barnes carries all the furniture out into the yard and vacuums the house from top to bottom. Then he carries the tables and chairs and beds back into the house and plonks himself down on the sofa. Spring Cleaning is over for another year.

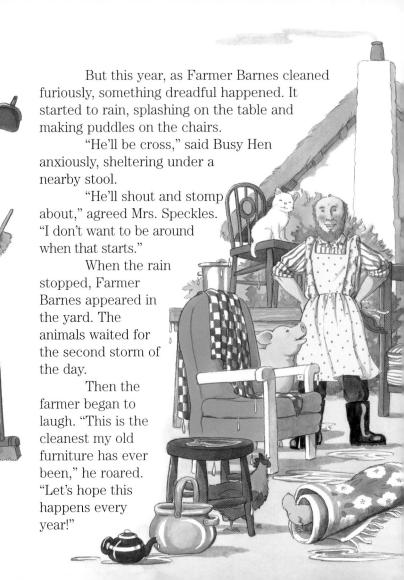

But this year, as Farmer Barnes cleaned furiously, something dreadful happened. It started to rain, splashing on the table and making puddles on the chairs.

"He'll be cross," said Busy Hen anxiously, sheltering under a nearby stool.

"He'll shout and stomp about," agreed Mrs. Speckles. "I don't want to be around when that starts."

When the rain stopped, Farmer Barnes appeared in the yard. The animals waited for the second storm of the day.

Then the farmer began to laugh. "This is the cleanest my old furniture has ever been," he roared. "Let's hope this happens every year!"

Lala Lamb's Singing Soirée

One morning after breakfast, the animals were surprised to hear someone banging a stick on the rain barrel.

"Excuse me!" called a little voice.

It was little Lala Lamb. "This evening," she said, "I am holding a *soirée* in the small barn. There will be singing (from me) and all other animals are asked to perform."

Harold the horse asked what everyone else was wondering. "What's a swaray?" he asked. "Will we all have to hold it?"

"No," laughed Lala. "A *soirée* is a kind of musical party. It will start at seven o'clock."

By the end of the day, Farmer Barnes was very worried about his animals. He had come across Biggy Pig making the most extraordinary noise behind the pig sty. He had seen Busy Hen skipping about in a very strange way. As for Harold the horse, Farmer Barnes could hardly believe his ears when he heard Harold mooing and clucking over the stable door. He didn't know that Harold was doing his impressions.

That evening, everyone gathered in the small barn and the *soirée* began. It was wonderful! As a Grand Finale, everyone sang the Farm Song:

Oh, Farmer Barnes he had a farm,
Ee-i-ee-i-o!
And on that farm lived Biggy Pig,
Ee-i-ee-i-o!
With a grunt, snort here,
And a grunt, snort there,
Here a grunt, there a snort,
Everywhere a grunt, snort!
Farmer Barnes he had a farm,
Ee-i-ee-i-o!

Can you sing the rest?

Where's Duchess's Hat?

After a few blustery days, Farmer Barnes found he had a lot of repairs to attend to on Windytop Farm.

With so much to think about, it's not surprising that Farmer Barnes wasn't concentrating by the time he was doing his last repair job of the day … putting Scary Scarecrow upright again in the top field. Scary was called Scary because he wasn't! He was the friendliest-looking scarecrow you've ever seen, and birds from miles around used to come and perch on his hat.

Farmer Barnes was just about to walk away, when he saw that Scary no longer had his hat. The farmer looked around. Aha! Farmer Barnes spotted a straw hat under the hedge and hurried to scoop it up and plonk it on Scary's head. It looked fine.

But back in the farmyard, someone else was missing a hat! Duchess the cow had lost hers in the wind as well.

When Lala and Delilah found a handsome top hat lying under a gate, they brought it straight back to Duchess, full of pride.

Seeing their eager little faces, Duchess hadn't the heart to be cross. She rather liked her jaunty new headgear, but all the other animals laughed until their sides ached.

Duchess smiled and set off to visit a certain scarecrow. As she passed the duckpond, she had one last look at herself. "Maybe it's not really *me*," she said, "but a stylish cow like me can carry anything off!"

The Pie Contest

One autumn day, Farmer Barnes tried to lift a bag of grain that was simply too heavy—and dropped it on his foot. He gave a yell and hobbled off to call the doctor.

"I don't want you to put any weight on that foot for a week," said the doctor firmly. "Let your friends take the strain for a while. It's high time you had a rest."

Farmer Barnes knew the doctor was right. His foot was far too painful to walk on. He was just beginning to wonder how he would manage as far as food was concerned, when his visitors started to arrive, one by one.

First Mrs. Mannheim from the next farm brought him one of her extra special chocolate-marshmallow pies. Half an hour later, Miss Florence

Fong brought a lemon-orange-and-pineapple pie, with caramel cream. Later that day, Mr. Baxter from the bakery came around with a maple-and-walnut-banana-and-meringue pie, and the doctor herself dropped by with a wholemeal-muesli-oatmeal-and-date pie.

"Sorry!" she laughed. "It's a bit solid. But it will do you good!"

That evening, Annie came in from the yard. "I couldn't get here before," she said, "but I have made you a pie to keep you going. Oh dear, I can see you've already got lots of beautiful fancy pies. Mine is just plain apple, I'm afraid."

"A plain apple pie is just what I feel like. I can always rely on you, Annie." said Farmer Barnes. He enjoyed his apple pie. Can you guess who enjoyed all the other ones?

Farmer Barnes Goes to Town

While Farmer Barnes was resting his injured foot, Annie looked after the farm, and she did it very well.

One morning, when Annie was feeding the ducks, there came a grumbling and a shouting from Farmer Barnes' open bedroom window.

"Oh, I wonder what the matter is," cried Annie, hoping the farmer hadn't dropped something else on his foot.

Dymphna Duck quacked loudly. She knew exactly what was going on. When Farmer Barnes went to town, he liked to look a bit smarter than usual. And the grumbling and shouting were because he always got cross with the fiddly little buttons on his best shirt.

At last Farmer Barnes was ready and set off for town.

"Didn't he look smart?" Annie said to Mrs. Speckles. "I expect he was going to the bank."

But when Farmer Barnes arrived home later that day, he was carrying a big box and looking anxious. He marched straight over to Annie and pushed the box toward her.

"Just wanted to say thank you," he said gruffly, "for all your hard work, you know. Don't know what we'd have done without you."

Annie went pink and peeped into the box. For a few seconds she was speechless. Then she pulled out the prettiest hat you've ever seen.

Busy Hen was doing a little dance of joy. She had hopes of her own for Annie and Farmer Barnes!

A Name for a Newcomer

Each year, lots of babies were born on Windytop Farm. Farmer Barnes liked to give names to them all, and he was pretty good at remembering them, too.

But one year, there were so many babies, he had to struggle to think of new names for all of them. To make things simpler, Farmer Barnes worked out his own system. He decided to give the chicks names beginning with C, like Charlie and Caroline. The lambs had names beginning with L, like Lucy and Lawrie, and so on.

It was when he came to the ducklings that Farmer Barnes had problems. He simply could not think of twenty-four names beginning with D, especially as several other animals on the farm already had D-names.

By the end of the week, Farmer Barnes had twenty-three names, but he was well and truly stuck on the last one. It so happened that the next day, Farmer Barnes' niece paid him a surprise visit, bringing along her baby daughter.

The baby loved seeing the animals. Last of all, Farmer Barnes took her to the duckpond.

"Here," he said, "is my biggest problem. What would be a good name for a duck, Rosie?"

Rosie didn't hesitate. "Duck!" she cried.

Farmer Barnes laughed out loud. "You know," he said, "that's not such a bad idea!"

The Sunset Race

With so many baby animals on Windytop Farm, the older animals were busy night and day keeping an eye on them. As the babies grew older, they were likely to wander off into the fields—but still not able to find their way home again. Evening after evening, Harold clip-clopped up the lane, calling to all the chicks and ducklings and goslings who had strayed from the yard.

One evening, Busy Hen called all the little ones together for a Serious Talk. She told them about fast cars, foxes, hawks, and hunters, until they all looked anxious.

"In future," said Busy Hen, "you must all stick together. There's safety in numbers."

At first, everything was fine. But one evening, the little ones didn't come home! Biggy Pig set off to find them and soon came across them in the Top Field.

"It's too far to walk home," explained one little duckling. "We're tired. Our little legs won't walk that far!"

"Oh, so you won't be able to take part in the Special Sunset Race, then?" sighed Biggy Pig.

"What race?" squeaked the little ones. "We're ready!"

"The winner is the first one back to the farmyard," said Biggy. "Ready? Set! Go!"

Those bad babies ran off as fast as their legs would carry them—every night from then on!

Biggy Pig's Dancing Lesson

Busy Hen was very busy these days. She was giving all the new chicks and ducklings dancing lessons—and one or two older birds were joining in as well.

"But why, Busy Hen? Why is everyone so keen on dancing now?" asked Harold the horse.

The dancing teacher looked mysterious. "You never know," she said, "when there might be some kind of … well … party or something."

One morning, just as her class had

finished, Busy Hen heard a strange sound coming from the pig sty.

"Pssssst! Pssssst!"

"What's the matter, Biggy?" asked Busy Hen. "Have you lost your voice?"

"No!" whispered the pig. "I just didn't want the other animals to hear. I wanted to talk to you about having private dancing lessons. I'd be too embarrassed to join one of your classes."

"You can't learn in your sty," said Busy Hen. "It's too small. Come out into the meadow."

And that's why the smallest chick, opening one sleepy eye at midnight, saw a wonderful sight. It was a pig, dancing in front of the huge harvest moon, and dancing beautifully.

A Wife for Farmer Barnes

These days, Annie seemed to be helping out more and more on the farm. Busy Hen kept her beady eyes open. She was sure that it was just a matter of time before the farmer asked Annie to marry him.

But days passed. Weeks passed. The weather grew colder. But nothing happened.

"What's the matter with the man?" muttered Busy Hen.

"Well, it's tricky for a chap," said Cackle. "You can't go rushing into these things."

"Well, you would say that, wouldn't you?" retorted Busy Hen. "You never did get up the courage to ask me to marry you. I had to do it!"

"I can't see Annie saying anything to Farmer Barnes, though," said Cackle.

On this occasion, Cackle, as so often, was completely wrong. One day, Annie marched into the yard with a Christmas tree under one arm and a box of trimmings under the other.

"It will be Christmas soon," said Annie, "and I can't bear the thought of you being all by yourself. I've waited long enough for you to say something, Fred, but I can see I'm just going to have to do it myself. It's high time you got married."

"But…" said Farmer Barnes, looking pink and happy at the same time.

"Yes, I mean me," laughed Annie, but she suddenly wasn't able to say another word!

"At last!" smiled Busy Hen.

Tree Trouble

When it is windy on Windytop Farm, as you know, it is very windy. One night, the animals covered their ears as they snuggled down in their straw, for a gale was blowing.

It wasn't until the next day that the full extent of the storm damage was obvious. A great tree had fallen across the farmyard, just missing the henhouse and barricading Harold in his stable. Of course, this wasn't the first time that a tree had been blown down on Windytop Farm, but this one had done dreadful damage as it fell.

Farmer Barnes was almost in tears as he looked at the scene in the farmyard. All he could think about was the time it would take and the money it would cost to put everything right again.

Just then Annie arrived and looked around.

"Well," she said, "that was lucky!"

"Lucky?" said Farmer Barnes faintly. "How can you call this lucky?"

Annie was smiling. "Not a single animal was hurt," she said, "and neither were you, Fred. I call that very lucky indeed."

Farmer Barnes grinned. "You're right," he said, "as always. Don't worry, Harold, we'll soon have you free. We'll be straight by Christmas!"

Buzz, Buzz!

Christmas had come at last to Windytop Farm, and all the animals were enjoying it enormously.

Duchess was given a new hat (it was one of Annie's old ones, but it looked very fine trimmed with some new ribbon). Harold became the proud owner of a sign with his name on it above the stable door.

There was something for everyone. Only Biggy Pig wasn't feeling on top of the world. At first he thought maybe the plum pudding was disagreeing with him. But gradually, the pig realized what was annoying him. There was a strange buzzing sound very near his left ear.

Buzz! Buzz! Buzz!

Biggy thought of all the obvious answers, but he was

pretty sure that it wasn't a bee or one of those things that buzzed in Farmer Barnes' kitchen. Then, just as Biggy felt he couldn't stand the buzzing any longer, along came Pompom the cat.

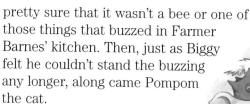

"So you've got it, Biggy!" she cried. She pounced into a corner of Biggy's sty and came out with ...

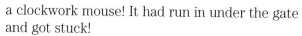

a clockwork mouse! It had run in under the gate and got stuck!

"Thank you, Pig!" purred Pompom. "And Merry Christmas!"

"And to you, Pompom," replied Biggy. "And a very peaceful New Year to all of us," he smiled, looking meaningfully at the mouse.

"*Buzz! Buzz!*" said the mouse. And what that meant is anybody's guess!

Annie Holds the Fort

No sooner had Christmas come and gone than it was lambing time again on Windytop Farm. Night after night, Farmer Barnes stayed up with his sheep, making sure that the little woolly lambs came safely into the world. By the end of it all, he was exhausted.

"Why don't you visit your sister for a couple of days?" suggested Annie. "I can hold the fort."

It just shows how tired the farmer was that he didn't even argue. Next morning, he rattled off in his old truck.

Annie set to work. She wanted everything to go well while Farmer Barnes was away. But everything that could go wrong, did go wrong. Annie tripped and dropped all the eggs. She fell against the henhouse, making a hole in the roof.

Busy Hen looked in dismay at the mess.
She couldn't bear the idea of Farmer Barnes
being cross with Annie, so she had a few sharp
words with the other animals. As the hens
frowned in concentration, trying to lay an extra
morning egg, Scraggles did his duty and ate up
all the eggy mess on the ground.

Meanwhile, Annie mended the henhouse
roof so it was as good as new.

When Farmer Barnes came back
late the next day, he smiled at the
peaceful sight that met his eyes.

"There's never trouble when you're
around, Annie," he said. And he didn't
hear Annie's reply because the hens
suddenly all started talking at once and
completely drowned out her words.

Don't Be Shy, Little Pig!

Biggy Pig was quite worried about Little Pig. "I know lots of youngsters are shy," Biggy told his friend Harold the horse, "but Little Pig won't say a word. He just turns pink—I mean, pinker than a pig usually is—and tries to hide his head in the straw. What am I to do with him?"

"It's natural for a youngster to feel shy," said Harold comfortingly.

"But Little Pig is growing up," said Biggy Pig. "He should have grown out of his shyness by now."

Yes, Little Pig was now a fine young pig, almost as big as Biggy.

Then, one day, Farmer Barnes brought a new lady pig to Windytop Farm. Her name was Philomena.

It was clear that Little Pig was very taken with Philomena. But he was so shy, he couldn't say a word to her.

"I simply don't know what to do," Biggy Pig told Harold. "I'm almost ashamed of the young pig. Goodness me, in my young day if a pretty young pig like Philomena came along, I was chatting to her in no time."

But the very next day, as Philomena

trotted across the farmyard, Biggy Pig was astonished to hear a loud voice just behind him. "Look out!" It was Little Pig! Philomena heard Little Pig's cry and managed to skip away just in time as a ladder came crashing down.

Well, after that, Little Pig never did say a lot, but he and Philomena have been very happy together ever since. And Biggy Pig has been quieter…

The Old Tractor

Farmer Barnes shook his head. "It's no use, Annie," he said. "I must be sensible. This old tractor will always be more trouble than it is worth. I shall call the scrap dealer to come and take it away."

For the next few days, the animals noticed that Farmer Barnes often went to look at the old tractor. He remembered so well how proud he was when his father taught him to drive it. Selling the tractor was like losing an old friend.

At last the day came when the tractor was taken away. The farmer hurried off to look at his sheep without saying a word.

A few days later, when Annie and Farmer Barnes were working in the fields, the farmer paused and looked up. "Annie," he said, "I went to town this morning and bought you a little something. I'm sorry I didn't think of it before."

As she opened the little box, Annie cried out with pleasure. It was an engagement ring. "But how could you afford…?" she began … and stopped. "Oh, Fred," she said, "you shouldn't have sold your tractor for me."

"You're worth it," said the farmer, smiling.

That afternoon, a truck arrived at the farm. The farmer was amazed when he saw on the back of the truck—his old tractor!

"That's my present to you, Fred," said Annie.

"I'm a lucky man, Annie," he said gruffly, as he went to greet the driver.

Moonlight Serenade

Windytop Farm is always a busy place, but in the days leading up to Farmer Barnes' wedding, it was incredibly busy. The ceremony was taking place in the nearby town, but all the guests were coming back to the farm afterwards.

Although Farmer Barnes was not a man to spend money idly, he was determined to have a wonderful wedding.

All week people were coming and going—with food, flowers, presents, and mysterious packages of all kinds. The animals tried not to get in the way.

The night before the wedding, Busy Hen could see Farmer Barnes pacing inside the farmhouse.

"He needs a good night's sleep," said Busy Hen. "Whatever can be the matter?"

"I know what it is," replied Cackle. "He's anxious about tomorrow. He'll be fine if he once gets to sleep."

"Then we must help him," said Busy Hen. And she called together all the animals. "Lala Lamb will sing the solo," she said. "Now, everyone, one, two, three!"

The animals sang beautifully, but Farmer Barnes looked out at once.

"What's that noise?" he cried.

Busy Hen smiled. "He'll feel better now he's had a shout at someone," she said. And she was right.

A Windytop Wedding

Farmer Barnes was up bright and early on his wedding morning. By half past nine, all the important jobs were done, and Farmer Barnes went indoors to get ready. When he came out again, he was hardly recognizable. All the animals watched as he climbed into his old truck and rumbled off down the lane.

"He's gone!" cried Busy Hen, scuttling around the barnyard as fast as she could. "We haven't got much time. Come on!" And all the animals dashed into action. The hens fluttered off to collect wild rose-petals from the hedges. Pompom the cat, who had clever little paws, tied bows on all the lady animals and helped Duchess to get her hat straight.

156

When everyone was ready, the animals hurried to hide, for they could hear the sound of a battered old truck coming down the lane.

The truck stopped in front of the farmhouse. Farmer Barnes got out, with a big smile on his face, and walked around to open the other door. The new Mrs. Barnes got out of the truck, and she looked absolutely beautiful.

"Everyone else will be here in a minute, darling," said the farmer, "but I'm looking forward to life being like this. Just you and me."

"Now!" cried Busy Hen, and the animals ran to congratulate the couple.

"Not *just* you and me," laughed Annie.

Arthur's Ark

One spring day, a party of schoolchildren visited Windytop Farm. Their teacher had arranged it with Fred and Annie Barnes a few weeks before. On the day of the visit, it was cloudy and quite cold. As Farmer Barnes had feared, there was a lot of mud everywhere. He was pleased to see, as the children climbed out of their minibus, that they all had sensible boots on their feet—except for one little boy.

"Arthur joined us from another school this week," said the teacher. "He's a wizz with his wheelchair and he's really looking forward to seeing the animals."

But Arthur didn't see very much of the farm. There were all sorts of steps and obstacles to stop him getting around.

"I'm so very sorry," said Annie. "We'll have to change things around here. Everyone should be able to visit Windytop Farm and see everything they want to see."

That night, as they had their supper, Farmer Barnes told Annie, "I'm going to make Arthur a present to show how sorry we are."

So the farmer went into his workshop and made lots of little wooden animals and a wooden ark. But when Arthur opened the package, he said, "Thank you very much, but it was pigs and sheep and things I really wanted to see."

Farmer Barnes understood. He hurried off to make models of all the farm animals. This time, Arthur beamed. "It's almost as good as seeing around the farm," he said.

"We'll make sure you can do just that next time," promised Annie and Farmer Barnes.

The Moon Pig

Biggy Pig was waiting impatiently for his breakfast. Where was Annie?

A few minutes later, he heard the clanking of buckets, and Farmer Barnes looked over the door of the sty. "Here's your breakfast, old friend," he said. "Sorry it's a bit late, but I don't want Annie overdoing things."

Little Pig heard everything Farmer Barnes said, and he began to wonder out loud about what was happening on Windytop Farm.

160

"It's very mysterious," said Little Pig, "and my dear Philomena agrees with me."

"What is?" yawned Biggy.

"The eggs not being collected on time," said Little Pig. "And Annie wearing Farmer Barnes' clothes—I think that's very odd."

"I think she's got too fat for her clothes," said Biggy Pig, who knew a thing or too about getting fat.

"It's still strange," said Little Pig. "And then there's the Moon Pig. When the Moon Pig turns blue, that means strange and wonderful things are going to happen. And the Moon Pig has been blue all this week."

"It's the time of year," said Biggy carelessly.

But that night, Little Pig whispered to the moon. "I don't care what Biggy says. Something strange and wonderful *is* going to happen. And it's going to happen soon."

You'll Never Believe It!

One morning, Little Pig scuttled around the farmyard and skidded to a halt in front of Dymphna the duck.

"I know what it is!" he panted. "I know why everything's been strange around here recently. I just heard Annie and Farmer Barnes talking. You'll never believe it!"

He whispered in her ear.

"You're right," said Dymphna. "I don't believe a word of it."

So Little Pig hurried on to have a word with Duchess the cow.

"Nonsense, young pig!" cried Duchess.

Feeling pretty desperate now, Little Pig ran to tell Harold the horse.

"I'm sure that can't be right," said Harold.

Little Pig was sitting sadly on a bale of straw when Busy Hen came by.

"What's the matter, Little Pig?" she asked.

"I know a really big secret," said Little Pig. "I've told everyone, and they don't believe it."

"Well, you haven't told me," said Busy Hen.

So Little Pig whispered his secret. And Busy Hen nodded.

"I've known," she said, "for ages. All we have to do is wait."

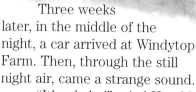

Three weeks later, in the middle of the night, a car arrived at Windytop Farm. Then, through the still night air, came a strange sound.

"It's a baby!" cried Harold.

"But…" quacked Dymphna.

"But…" mooed Duchess.

"BUT…" they cried together, "that means you were right, Little Pig. And it's *wonderful* news."

And Farmer Barnes leaned out of a window and said, *"Ssshhh!"*

Kitten Tales

Meet the Little Kittens!

Here are five little kittens who just love to get up to mischief! Come and join them!

Honeybun

Rolypoly

Tiger Tail

Mopsy

Fluffy

Where's That Kitten?

When a mother cat has five little kittens to take care of, she certainly has her paws full!

One morning, Mamma Cat was busy giving her babies their breakfast. "One bowl of porridge for you, and one for you, and one for you, and one for you, and one... Just a minute, where's that kitten?" The fifth little kitten was nowhere to be seen.

Mamma Cat looked everywhere. But there was no little kitten to be found.

"Now then," said Mamma Cat, "one of you kittens must know where your brother is."

"I don't know," mewed Fluffy.

"I haven't seen him at all," said Rolypoly.

168

"Nor have I, Mamma," said Mopsy.

But when Mamma Cat turned to her fourth kitten, it was as plain as could be that he knew something.

"He's gone on a climbing adventure," said Honeybun.

Mamma Cat frowned and sighed. "Really? I hope he took an oxygen mask. In really high places, the air is very thin. It would be difficult for a little kitten to breathe without extra oxygen. And that would be dangerous."

Before Honeybun could say another word, they all heard a plaintive little sound.

"Help!" called someone from a really high place. "Help! Meow! Help!"

Mamma Cat didn't need to look around. She reached straight up to the top of the closet and scooped up one frightened kitten.

"Oh," said poor Tiger Tail, "my climbing *up* is very good, but my climbing *down* isn't. And, of course, without oxygen…"

"I have heard," smiled Mamma Cat, "that porridge is just as good as oxygen in some situations. No more climbing, please, until after breakfast!"

Tiger Tail Trouble

Some little kittens just can't help getting into trouble. They try as hard as they can to be good. They don't mean to throw pudding over visiting cats—but still Great Aunt Flora has to wash her whiskers. They run as fast as they can to get home in time for supper, but still Mamma Cat is waiting grimly on the doorstep with a plate of burnt sausages. Tiger Tail was a kitten just like that.

One morning, Tiger Tail looked at the calendar and saw that it was Mother's Day. Fluffy, Rolypoly, Mopsy, and Honeybun all had little presents for Mamma Cat.

Tiger Tail felt guilty. Quietly, he slipped out to buy a present.

Oh dear! Even when he was trying to do something good, Tiger Tail got into trouble. First he got caught on a thornbush and tore his

trousers. Then, as he was looking to see if his undies were showing, he fell into a puddle. And as he tried to clean himself up, the penny he had been clutching rolled out of his paw and fell into a stream by the road.

It was late and beginning to get dark as Tiger Tail arrived home. Mamma Cat was waiting anxiously at the door as one tired and muddy little kitten threw himself into her arms and sobbed out the whole sorry story.

But Mamma Cat gave him a big kiss and squeezed him tight. "The best present of all is knowing that you are safe and sound, Tiger Tail!"

The Great Escape

Lots of kittens like to collect something. It may be stamps, or shells, or leaves. At school, all the little kittens loved to show each other their latest finds.

Even Tiger Tail, who preferred climbing trees to collecting things, had a very interesting box of feathers he'd found on his many fur-raising adventures.

Only George did not have a collection. It seemed that everything he was interested in was already collected by someone else. Then, one morning, as he was digging in the garden for his granny, he had an idea. "There is one thing I am really interested in," he said to himself. "I'll start collecting today."

But George decided he would not tell anyone about his collection yet. He put it in his locker at school to keep it safe.

Unfortunately, George didn't know that the lockers were

172

cleaned every week. And this week, the cleaner left the door ever so slightly open...

Next morning, Mrs. Mumbles, the teacher, was busy showing the class some number work when she suddenly gave a great shriek.

"Oooooh!" she cried. "Something slithery has squiggled down my neck!"

At the same moment, Mopsy jumped onto her desk. "Something wiggly is sitting on my book!"

In no time at all, everyone was shouting at once. Only George was calm. "Stop!" he cried. "You'll frighten them!"

At that moment, all the kittens and Mrs. Mumbles turned to look at George.

"It's just my collection of worms," he explained. "There are seventeen of them."

It took ages for the class to find all the wiggly worms. Can you help them?

$$4 - 1 = 3$$
$$1 - 4 =$$

Bella's Birthday

Most kittens are friendly and fun, but once in a while you may meet a kitten who is just a little too big for her boots. When Bella invited all the other kittens to her birthday party, she made sure they knew it would be the biggest and best party ever.

Bella lived in a very grand house. When the kittens arrived, she greeted them at the door.

"Do come in," she said. "But please wipe your paws carefully. You poorer kittens may not be used to fine carpets."

It would have been a lovely party, if Bella had not tried to show off all the time. Even the magician, Mr. Kat, got tired of her comments.

"I know how that's done,"
she said loudly, as he produced
a bunch of flowers from a hat.

"Now, listen to me!" called
Bella, at the end of the show.
"Come into the garden to
watch me being photographed."

The kittens trooped outside,
where Melinda Felini, the famous
photographer, was waiting.

"Perhaps you'd like to hold
these giant balloons, Bella," she
suggested.

Up, up, and away went
the birthday kitten!

Some say that Mr. Kat used magic to
make that wind blow! Some say that Bella was a
kind and quiet kitten ever after.

The Package Problem

One autumn day, Mamma Cat sneezed and sniffled as she sat in her chair.

"You stay inside where it's warm and we'll do everything," said the little kittens kindly.

"Tiger Tail and Honeybun can take this package to Farmer Feather," said Mamma Cat. "It's his birthday."

The package wasn't heavy, but it was an awkward shape.

Outside, the two kittens realized they had a big problem. The wind seemed to love that package!

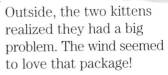

176

First it blew on it so hard that Tiger Tail and Honeybun could hardly hold on. Then, as they staggered into the barnyard, the wind played one last trick. it caught hold of the string on the package and wrapped it around the gatepost, so that it took Tiger Tail ten minutes to untangle it.

Farmer Feather was delighted with his present. It was too large to go through the doorway, so he opened it in the yard.

"Be careful," warned Honeybun. "The wind seems to want to play with it. It might fly away!"

But Farmer Feather laughed. "Oh no," he said. "The wind can play with it every day and it will never fly away. It's the most beautiful weather vane I've ever seen!"

Curious Kittens

Tiger Tail kicked at a leaf lying on the path. "I'm bored," he said. "We've played all our usual games."

"Let's go down to Farmer Feather's farm," suggested Honeybun. "We can see what his weather vane looks like on the farmhouse."

They came across Farmer Feather working on his tractor in a field before they reached the farmhouse. "Yes, you can go and look," he said, "but don't open the barn door."

Down at the farmhouse, the kittens thought the weather vane looked lovely.

"Now what?" asked Rolypoly. Tiger Tail didn't answer. He was looking at the barn.

The other kittens looked too.

"I wonder what is in there," said Rolypoly.

Those five naughty kittens crept up to the barn door. They tried to peek in through the slats of wood, but they couldn't see anything.

"All right," said Rolypoly. "Let's open the door just a tiny, tiny bit."

Fluffy stood on tiptoes to open the latch.

Squawk! Cluck! Quark! The kittens tumbled backward as twenty fluttering fowls rushed out of the barn.

Just at that moment Farmer Feather came home. He was not happy.

"You'll have to help me catch them," he said.

When they had finished, the kittens were out of breath but smiling. It had been lots of fun catching those chickens!

The Pawprint Puzzle

For one whole week, the little kittens had been cooped up inside, while outside the wind blew and the snow fell. The kittens spent a lot of time pretending to be detectives.

At last Mamma Cat looked out and said, "The snow has stopped, and the sun is shining. Put on your mittens and go outside."

Tiger Tail was ready first. He slipped out of the back door with a smile. "Come and find me!" he called.

When the other little kittens opened the front door, Tiger Tail was nowhere to be seen, but a nice clear set of prints led away from the back door and up to the gate.

But there the prints
stopped. The little kittens puzzled
and puzzled, but Tiger Tail seemed to
have vanished into thin air!

Suddenly, they heard a
giggle. It was Tiger Tail!

"Foiled again, detectives!"
he chortled. "It's simple. I walked
to the gate, and then I walked
back again … backward! I put
my paws in the prints I'd
made before. Ha! Ha!"

Splat! A snowball hit
Tiger Tail on the nose,
and for the next hour,
the great detectives
had lots of fun taking
their revenge!

181

The Picnic Pie

One sunny day, Mamma Cat had a surprise for the little kittens. "We're going into the woods for a picnic," she said. "And if you make some sandwiches, I'll make a special pie for us."

"Can it be a cherry pie, Mamma?" asked Tiger Tail.

"Oh no, Mamma," chorused Fluffy and Honeybun. "We like apple pie best."

But Mopsy and Rolypoly voted for plum pie!

"What am I going to do with you?" sighed Mamma Cat. "We'll ask your father what he likes best."

Father Cat smiled at Mamma Cat. "Well, I don't mind," he said. "All your pies are delicious!"

"Then I will decide," said Mamma Cat.

An hour later, the picnic was ready. It was lovely walking through the trees and even nicer when they sat down to munch their sandwiches. Then it was time for the famous pie. Mamma Cat cut slices for everyone and handed them out on paper plates.

"Just don't say anything until you've tasted it," she said.

Tiger Tail took a bite. "It is cherry!" he cried. "Thank you, Mamma."

"But there are some apples in it too," grinned Fluffy and Honeybun.

"And plums," said Mopsy and Rolypoly.

"It's a mixed-fruit pie," smiled Mamma, "with something for everyone."

"You know," said Father Cat, "*This* is the kind of pie I like best!"

It's a Monster!

One day, Mrs. Mumbles, the little kittens' teacher, asked them to practise reading, but the kittens didn't want to sit still.

After lots of interruptions, Mrs. Mumbles rolled up her sleeves and pretended to look very serious. "Now," she said, "while you read your books, I must straighten out the supply room."

"No, no!" cried the kittens. "We can do it!" They had secretly all wanted to find out what was kept behind the supply room door.

"All right," said Mrs. Mumbles. "But I want you little kittens to be very, very careful. Some supplies can be dangerous."

"Maybe there are spiders in there," shuddered Bella.

"Or something smelly," said George.

"Yes, yes," interrupted Honeybun quickly. "But I've thought of something even worse it might be. It might be … a *monster*!"

"They do often live in small dark places," agreed Tiger Tail. "We're going to have to be very, very careful."

So the bravest kittens—Tiger Tail, Mopsy, and George—crept into the supply room. It was very dark. As they reached the back of the room, George fell over a bucket. A mop and a swimming towel went flying, and an old drum went *BOOM!*

The three brave kittens had never run so fast in their lives. "It *is* a monster!" they shouted. "It's got floppy hair and flappy arms and it goes *BOOM!* Shut the door quickly!"

Mrs. Mumbles came along to find a whole class of kittens reading very nicely from their books. She gave a small smile to herself. Well, well. So the mop-and-bucket monster trick had worked again this year!

Now Remember...

Mamma Cat looked at the clock. She had to mail her letters now or it would be too late.

"You are old enough to take care of yourselves for a few minutes," she told the four little kittens. "But promise you won't open the door for anyone, except Father, of course."

"We promise!" said the kittens. So Mamma Cat put on her coat and hurried off to the post office.

She had only been gone for a few minutes when there was a tapping at the door.

"Let me in! Let me in!" called Fluffy. She had just come home from her piano lesson.

The kittens looked at each other. "We promised not to open the door," said Rolypoly.

"But it's starting to rain," cried Mopsy. "Poor Fluffy will get wet!"

Then Tiger Tail had one of his Good Ideas. "We promised not to open the door," he said, "but we didn't promise anything at all about the window!"

And that is why, when Mamma Cat and Father Cat arrived home at almost the same moment a little while later, they found Fluffy's little legs waving out of the window, where she was well and truly stuck!

Fluffy was soon rescued, and Mamma Cat said she was sorry for forgetting her. Luckily, Mamma hadn't forgotten to buy some pastries for tea!

187

The Treehouse

The little kittens loved to climb trees, but they often got stuck!

"You kittens are just going to have to find some other way to have fun in the woods," said Father Cat. "One day I may be away when you need rescuing."

Suddenly, Mopsy got the tingling feeling that often means a Really Good Idea is about to arrive. "Quiet!" she called. "Let me think." The kittens did not have to wait long.

"We," said Mopsy grandly, "are going to build a treehouse."

The kittens cheered!

Tiger Tail and Honeybun set off at once for Farmer Feather's wood-shed to … well … *borrow* some of Farmer Feather's wood.

Considering that five little architects helped with the plans, and five little builders hoisted and hammered, and five little painters splished and sploshed, the treehouse was finished in an amazingly short time. It did look unlike any other treehouse you have ever seen, to be sure, but it was snug, and cheerful, and in a tree —what more could a kitten wish for?

The little kittens have decided to keep the treehouse a secret for now, but Father Cat is already very suspicious about the painty pawprints on his path. He wonders if they could have anything to do with the mysterious disappearance of Farmer Feather's ladder…

Oh, Pickles!

One morning, Mamma Cat received a letter. "Your cousin Pickles is coming to stay," she said, looking at her own five little kittens.

There was silence for a moment.

"Over my dead body!" cried Father Cat, leaping to his feet. "Do you remember last time? I had to replumb the bathroom, retile the kitchen, put up a new fence, and apologize to all the cats for miles around for things that kitten had done. I'm not going through all that again."

The little kittens agreed, but it was too late. Pickles was already on his way.

And the funny thing was that Pickles was not bad at all. He was polite to his uncle and aunt and he sat down quietly at the table.

"Well, Pickles," said Father Cat. "You really seem to have changed. You certainly made your presence felt last time you were here."

"Oh," smiled Pickles. "I was little then. I'm much more grown up now. Thank you for a lovely dinner. I think I'll go to bed early after my long journey."

Pickles stood up and turned away. Unfortunately, the tablecloth had been tucked in his belt. In one quick motion, the plates, the saucers, the casserole, and Mamma Cat's famous marmalade pudding hurtled across the room.

"Oh, Pickles!" cried Father Cat, Mamma Cat, and the five kittens, with tears of laughter rolling down their furry cheeks. "We were wrong! You haven't changed at all, have you?"

Ssssh!

One night, when all the Cat family was fast asleep, Tiger Tail woke up with a start. He was sure that he had heard something. He crept bravely out of bed and went to investigate.

But as Tiger Tail went out, the bedroom door closed with a loud *click*!

The next thing Tiger Tail knew, Fluffy was creeping along the hallway too.

"I thought I heard a noise like a *click*," she whispered.

"That was me," said Tiger Tail. "Ssssh!"

But Fluffy had already knocked an apple out of the fruit bowl. *Thud!*

Seconds later, Rolypoly tiptoed out to meet them.

"I thought I heard a
thud," he said.

"That was me," said Fluffy. "Ssssh!"

But Rolypoly had already bumped into a
bookshelf. A book fell over with a *wumph*!

Almost at once, Mopsy crept out to join
the other kittens.

"I thought I heard a sort of
wumph noise," she whispered.

"That was me," said
Rolypoly. "Ssssh!"

But Rolypoly skidded on
the floor and hit the wall with
a *thwack*!

Honeybun came
creeping along to join them.
They all listened. There
was a quiet munching
sound coming from the
kitchen. It was Father Cat
with a huge sandwich!

The Lost Letter

One wet morning, as Honeybun was running down the lane, he met the mailcat, Mr. String.

"Will you take this letter to your mother?" asked Mr. String.

Honeybun took the letter and carefully put it in his pocket. He would give it to Mamma Cat that afternoon after school.

But when he came home from school that day, Honeybun forgot about the letter. And it was days before he wore his raincoat again and found it in the pocket.

The kitten felt dreadful. What if it was something important? He took the letter out of his pocket and read the big red writing on the front. "YOU ARE A WINNER!" it said. "CLAIM NOW OR LOSE YOUR PRIZE!"

Honeybun felt sick. He imagined the huge amount of money that his carelessness might have lost. His family would never forgive him.

All day Honeybun felt awful. It was as if he had a heavy weight in his tummy. After school, he took the letter straight to Mamma Cat.

"I'm sorry," he sobbed, as he explained.

Mamma Cat put her arm around her little one. "It was just a mistake, honey," she said. "Let's see what this silly thing is about."

Honeybun couldn't understand why Mamma Cat laughed when she read the letter.

"Well done!" she said, between giggles. "We would have won a lifetime's supply of Purple Fizz, and you know how we all hate that yucky drink. You saved us from being purple-fizzily flooded!"

195

Who's Who?

The little kittens had gone to see an exciting movie. When they got home, they could only think of one thing.

"Let's play spies!" suggested Tiger Tail.

"We'll need to disguise ourselves," said Mopsy. "Let's see what we can find!"

The kittens had a wonderful time playing spies that afternoon, until Mamma Cat and Father Cat came home from shopping.

"Who's been in my room, borrowing my clothes?" cried Mamma Cat.

"And who's been in my chest of drawers, borrowing *my* clothes?" yelled Father Cat.

"And someone's been in my sewing basket too,"

said Mamma Cat, looking at her mending things spread across the carpet.

"And my coveralls are missing," said Father Cat.

They soon found five very guilty-looking spies lurking in the kitchen.

"It's lucky you spies are in disguise," said Father Cat, trying not to smile. "If I knew which of you was which, I'd have to give you a serious talking-to."

The little kittens scampered off to put their disguises away. I'll bet you could tell which was which, couldn't you? But don't tell Father Cat!

197

Huggie's Hat

All the little kittens loved to visit Farmer Feather's farm. There were so many things to see and do there. And, of course, there was Huggie, too. Huggie had worked for Farmer Feather for more years than the little kittens could count. The kittens loved to hear his stories about life on the farm years ago.

One day, Huggie greeted them with a smile and a wave.

"I've got a job for you little kittens today," he said. "We need a new scarecrow in the top field. I thought you might want to make him for me. Here are some sticks to make him stand up straight.

198

You can fill these sacks with straw to make his head and body, and here are some old clothes to dress him in when you're finished. Have fun!"

The kittens loved making the scarecrow. When they were finished, they stepped back and looked at their creation. Huggie came in to have a look, too. "That's wonderful," he said, scratching his head. "He looks a little like me! Now you can take him into the field and push him into the ground."

But Fluffy was still frowning after Huggie had left.

"There's something missing," she said. "He needs a hat!"

"There wasn't a hat with the clothes," said Tiger Tail. Then all the kittens noticed that Huggie had left his battered old hat behind. It was perfect!

Later, the kittens started out for home.

"See you soon," called Huggie. "You haven't seen my hat around, have you?"

A Fishy Tale

One late summer day, Honeybun saw Farmer Feather going past in the lane. He was dressed rather strangely and carrying a long pole. Honeybun ran out to see where his friend was going.

"I'm off to the river to do some fishing," said Farmer Feather. "Would you like to come?"

Honeybun couldn't believe his furry little ears. He ran inside to tell Mamma right away.

"As long as you stay with Farmer Feather, that's fine," she said. "Bring us back a fish for our supper!"

Honeybun and Farmer Feather soon reached the riverbank. Farmer Feather set up his fishing rod and sat down.

Honeybun sat down, too. "What happens now?" he asked.

"We wait," said the farmer. "Ssssh!"

Honeybun waited.

"If you don't stop wriggling, you'll have to go home," said Farmer Feather.

"How much longer do we have to wait?" asked Honeybun.

"Who knows? An hour or two?"

Honeybun sat still for a moment. "I've just remembered I've got to go home," he said.

"What, no fish?" called Mamma Cat.

"It was hopeless," said Honeybun. "Farmer Feather kept talking, and he scared them all away!"

The Squiggly Thing

One morning, Rolypoly pushed his bowl away at breakfast. He climbed onto Mamma Cat's lap and whispered in her ear. He didn't want the other little kittens to hear.

"I've got a squiggly thing in my tummy!" he said.

"A squiggly thing?" said Mamma. "What have you been eating, Rolypoly?"

"Nothing," whispered her son. "It's just a very wriggly, squiggly thing."

Mamma Cat looked at him carefully.

"Is it wriggling and squiggling all the time?" she asked.

"No," said Rolypoly, "only when I think about my reading test."

Then Mamma Cat understood. Some of the little kittens had a reading test at school that

morning, and it was making Rolypoly nervous. The squiggly thing was just nervousness in his tummy.

"But Rolypoly," said Mamma, "you read beautifully. You just do your best on the test. That's all you can possibly do. And I will be proud of you no matter what."

Then Mamma Cat gave Rolypoly a big hug, and the little kitten found that the squiggly thing had wriggled right away.

That afternoon, the kittens all cheered Rolypoly. He got the highest mark of all, and Mamma was very proud.

Alfred to the Rescue

One morning, Father Cat started to paint the upstairs windows. The little kittens were playing in the garden. Just then, another kitten went past in the lane and waved to Mamma Cat's family. The kittens ignored him.

"Who was that?" asked Mamma Cat.

"Oh," said Fluffy, "that was Alfred. He's new at school."

"Why didn't you ask him to come and play?" asked Mamma. "I thought Alfred looked a little lonely."

Half an hour later, the kittens were playing an exciting game of chase-the-tail.

"Careful!" warned Father Cat, high up on his ladder.

But Tiger Tail, tearing around the corner of the house, didn't hear him. *Crash!* He knocked the ladder and Father Cat lost his footing. As he grabbed the top of the

window, his paint can sailed up into the air and landed on his head.

"Help!" cried Father Cat. "I can't see a thing!"

"Keep calm!" cried a voice from the lane. It was Alfred, and he took charge at once.

"I'm going to talk you down, Mr. Cat," he said. "Just do exactly what I say. Now move your right paw to the left.…"

In no time, Father Cat was safe. Everyone wanted to congratulate Alfred and be his friend.

"I'm glad you weren't hurt, Mr. Cat," said Alfred.

"Not hurt," giggled Mamma Cat, "but a lovely shade of lavender. It's very becoming, dear!"

Aunt Amelia

Mamma Cat was surprised when Mrs. Mumbles stopped her in the street one Saturday morning. Mrs. Mumbles was the little kittens' schoolteacher.

"I was just wondering, Mrs. Cat," said Mrs. Mumbles in sympathetic tones, "how your dear sister is now. The kittens have been so worried about her. I do understand that they find it hard to concentrate in class when she is on their minds."

"My sister?" said Mamma faintly.

"Yes," said Mrs. Mumbles, "the kittens' Aunt Amelia. I do hope there is good news."

"Excellent news," said Mamma Cat briskly. "She has made a remarkable recovery and went home this morning."

When Mamma Cat arrived home, she beamed at her kittens.

"My dears," she said, "Your Aunt Amelia, who has been so ill, is much better now and is coming to stay with us!"

The kittens looked at each other. They knew perfectly well that Tiger Tail and Honeybun had invented Aunt Amelia on the spur of the moment when they were faced with an extra-long spelling test.

"Oh, Mamma," said Mopsy. "I don't understand. How can Aunt Amelia visit? There isn't a real Aunt. We made her up, Mamma. I'm sorry."

"I know," said Mamma. "And if you naughty little kittens aren't very good over the next few weeks, Mrs. Mumbles will know too."

"We'll be good!" chorused the kittens.

Katie's Clock

Mamma Cat did her best to make sure that her little kittens were never late for school. Unfortunately, Katie Kitten, who lived nearby, was nearly always late. Her mother had not five but twelve little kittens to look after. It was not surprising that she often forgot to wind the clock, so it nearly always showed the wrong time.

When Mrs. Mumbles lost patience with poor Katie, who didn't have a watch, the little kitten decided to try something new.

208

For the rest of that week, Katie was on time. Mrs. Mumbles was very pleased. On Friday, she gave the class a test.

"I want absolute silence," she said. But it seemed that absolute silence was difficult to find. First one of Farmer Feather's tractors rumbled by. Then a dog barked.

"Don't be distracted, class," said Mrs. Mumbles. "I hope we'll have peace now."

But just then ... *drriiiiiiing! drriiiiiiing!* Mrs. Mumbles nearly jumped out of her fur.

"I'm sorry," said Katie. "I've been bringing my granny's alarm clock, so that I'm not late."

Later, the kittens told Mamma what had happened. Next morning, Katie was very happy. "Look!" she said. "A surprise present arrived last night. It's a watch!"

Can you guess who might have sent it?

209

Splish! Splash!

Mamma Cat sighed as she looked at the dirty dishes by the sink.

"We'll do it for you, Mamma," said Mopsy.

Mamma Cat was very tired, so she stopped listening to the warning voice in her head. She went into the living room and put her paws up. Soon she was fast asleep.

Fluffy and Rolypoly cleared the rest of the dishes from the kitchen table. Tiger Tail took charge of the sink … and turned on the water so hard that everyone was soaked. Mopsy squeezed a little too much dishwashing liquid into the sink.

"What lovely bubbles!" squealed Fluffy. "We could have a bubble-blowing contest!"

For ten minutes, the dishwashing was forgotten as five little kittens chased bubbles.

At last Honeybun began washing the dishes. Fluffy and Mopsy dried, and Rolypoly and Tiger Tail put the cups, plates, knives, forks, and spoons away.

The floor was fairly slippery by now, with all the spilled water and bubbles, so it wasn't really Rolypoly's fault when he fell over and a few things got broken.

When Mamma Cat came in a few minutes later, she suddenly felt much more tired than she had before.

"We can't understand why you don't like washing dishes, Mamma," cried the five little kittens. "We think it's lots of fun!"

The Pumpkin Prize

It was the time of year when the local Fruit and Vegetable Show was only weeks away. For more years than he cared to remember, Father Cat had tried to win the Pumpkin Prize. It was for the biggest, roundest, brightest orange pumpkin in the show. And for just as many years, the biggest, roundest, brightest orange pumpkin had been grown by Farmer Feather. Father Cat and Farmer Feather were the best of friends usually, but at this time of year, they were deadly rivals.

This year, the kittens had bought Father Cat a special book for his birthday. It was called *Expert Pumpkin Growing*. Father Cat read every word and managed to grow a really huge orange pumpkin.

Long before the show, he realized that his wheelbarrow would not be big enough to carry it, so he made a special little cart.

On the morning of the show, everyone helped Father Cat load the pumpkin.

"I'll open the gate," said Honeybun.

But opening the gate did not help. The pumpkin was much wider than the cart or the gate. It just would not go through.

"Oh dear, what a shame," said Father Cat. "It would probably have won the prize, but it will have to stay in the garden. Never mind."

Mamma Cat and the little kittens couldn't believe that Father Cat was taking it all so well. But then, they hadn't seen what he had just seen, far away in one of Farmer Feather's fields, had they?

The Christmas Kittens

It was the coldest, snowiest Christmas Mamma and Father Cat could remember. The five kittens loved it.

"This is perfect weather for Christmas," sighed Fluffy, gazing out of the window at the best snowcat she had made yet. "And there are only three days to go!" She couldn't keep a little squeak of excitement out of her voice.

"You know," said Mamma Cat, "we are very lucky to have such a nice, warm home at Christmastime, even if it is cold outside. Some cats and kittens are not so lucky. I think we should ask another family to join us on Christmas Day, to share our dinner."

"No!" said Father Cat. "Five little kittens squealing over their presents are enough!"

"No!" said Mopsy. "Strange kittens might break my new toys."

"No!" said Rolypoly. "Other kittens would eat my little mince pie."

"No!" said Tiger Tail. "If we have visitors, we'll have to be quiet."

"No!" said Honeybun. "It's fun with just us here."

"Well," said Fluffy, "I'm not sure it would be fun if we kept thinking about poor kittens who aren't so lucky."

"Well, if you put it like that…" muttered Father Cat.

So that was why there were eleven little kittens around the Christmas table that year. And everyone had the best Christmas ever!

A New Friend

The little kittens were not very happy when they heard that Great Aunt Florence was coming to stay.

"Remember," said Mamma Cat, "Great Aunt Florence is not a young cat. She will need peace and quiet more than anything else. Do you understand?"

"Yes, Mamma," said the little kittens, but they could feel their whiskers drooping. There would be no fun in the house at all while Great Aunt Florence was staying.

But when the elderly cat arrived, she wasn't at all like they had expected.

"Call me Flo!" she said. Flo wore lots and lots of beads and bangles (which dangled in her soup!) She used words that made Father Cat shudder and the little kittens giggle!

Still, the little kittens tried hard to be good and quiet. But after three days, Tiger Tail said, "Let's go right to the end of the orchard and have a good game of soccer!"

When Great Aunt Florence appeared suddenly, the kittens felt guilty. They had been being very noisy. But Flo's eyes were sparkling.

"Well, well, soccer!" she cried. "I was beginning to worry about you kittens. You were so good and quiet."

She took off her big hat and tossed it into a tree. Then she expertly kicked the ball right at her hat.

"GOAL!" she yelled.

A Terrible Tangle

Mamma Cat was knitting squares as if her life depended on it.

"The squares are going to be joined together," she told the kittens, "to make a big blanket. I'm making one, and Mrs. Willow is making one. I'm determined to finish first."

"Let us help you, Mamma!" said Fluffy. "You're sure to win then."

Mamma looked a little doubtful, but the kittens looked so eager, she agreed at last.

"I'm using yarn from some old sweaters you've outgrown," she said. "All you have to do is unravel them by pulling gently."

"We can do that!" cried the kittens.

But when Mamma Cat walked back into the room, she couldn't believe the sight that met her eyes. Bright yarn was crisscrossing the room in all directions. It was hanging from the lamp and twirling around the furniture.

"Oh no!" groaned Mamma Cat.

But when Tiger Tail saw how upset Mamma was, he said, "There will be a special prize for the kitten who winds up all of his or her ball first!"

Who do you think won? And who is in danger of undoing some of Mamma's hard work?

What's My Name?

One evening, Mamma Cat read the little kittens the funny story of Rumpelstiltskin. The next day, the little kittens were still thinking about the story.

"It was lucky the Queen managed to find out the name," said Mopsy. "She would never have been able to guess it."

"Nonsense!" cried Tiger Tail. "I bet I could have guessed it. You could see from the pictures that the little man looked just like someone who would be called Rumpelstiltskin."

"Is that so?" asked Mamma Cat. "So you could guess your father's name then?"

"But we know it," said Fluffy. "It's Charles."

"But his full name is Charles F. Cat," said Mamma. "What is the F.?"

"Now, now, we don't need to go into that," muttered Father Cat.

But the little kittens were curious now.

"Is it Ferdinand, Frederick, Francis, or Felix?" they asked.

"No," said Father Cat.

"Is it Floozle, Fenugreek, Fandangle, or Finklefog?" asked Tiger Tail.

"No!"

"Now, dear," said Mamma Cat. "It's a sweet name. After all, you did use it for one of your own children."

At that, the kittens burst out laughing. Can you guess Father Cat's full name now?

Open House

Mamma Cat sighed and looked at her appointment book. "I know what we're going to do," she said. "We've been invited out by lots of cats recently, and we must ask them to visit us in return. We'll have an Open Day. We can invite everyone at the same time. We'll call it an Open House."

"Good idea," mumbled Father Cat, who was munching a sandwich. "You arrange it, dear. Invite whoever you like."

"I certainly will," said Mamma Cat, "but you are going to have to fix the hinges on the front door. It feels very wobbly every time I open it. We can't have it coming off in a visitor's paw."

"I'll do it tonight," said Father Cat. But, you know, with one thing and another, Father Cat never did get around to fixing the door…

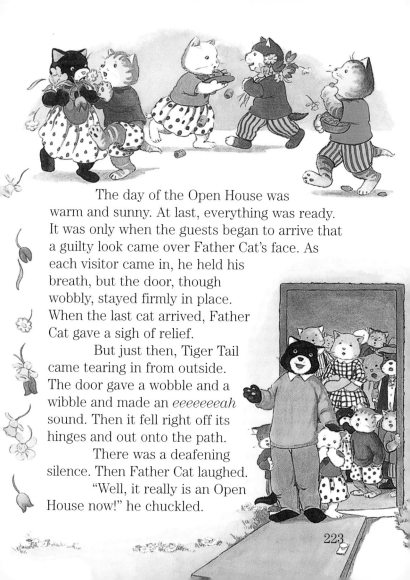

The day of the Open House was
warm and sunny. At last, everything was ready.
It was only when the guests began to arrive that
a guilty look came over Father Cat's face. As
each visitor came in, he held his
breath, but the door, though
wobbly, stayed firmly in place.
When the last cat arrived, Father
Cat gave a sigh of relief.

But just then, Tiger Tail
came tearing in from outside.
The door gave a wobble and a
wibble and made an *eeeeeeeah*
sound. Then it fell right off its
hinges and out onto the path.

There was a deafening
silence. Then Father Cat laughed.

"Well, it really is an Open
House now!" he chuckled.

223

The Honey Pot

One afternoon, Farmer Feather brought Mamma Cat a huge pot of honey. It was a pretty blue pot, filled to the brim with lovely golden honey from Farmer Feather's own bees.

When Tiger Tail saw the honey pot, he wanted to dip his little paw in right away.

"Just one little taste, Mamma!" he pleaded, but Mamma Cat was firm.

"I don't want sticky pawmarks all over the house," she said. "You can have some tomorrow."

But when she turned out the lights before bed that night, Mamma Cat herself couldn't resist taking a peek inside. And when she saw the golden honey, she dipped her paw just a little way into it. Mmmmm!

That night, one little kitten after another discovered that it was very hard to sleep without a taste of that honey. One by one, they crept into the kitchen and had just one—or maybe two—or maybe a few—tastes of the yummy sweet, sticky stuff. Even Father Cat slipped out of bed when the moon was high in the sky, and I'm sorry to say that he had quite a few tastes.

Next evening at supper, Mamma announced, "Now you can all have as much honey as you like on your bread and butter."

But strangely enough, no one wanted any!

Then Mamma smiled. "It's a good thing we all had a taste yesterday," she said, "because there isn't any left at all today!"

Three Little Kittens

One evening, as Mamma sat in her chair with her feet up, Tiger Tail rushed through and upset her cup of coffee all over the floor. Honeybun, who was not paying attention, ran into the room and skidded right into the puddle of coffee. He fell down with a bump and knocked over a vase. Fluffy, reading a book, walked through the mess and left wet pawprints all the way into the kitchen. Rolypoly tripped over Honeybun, and Mopsy, coming to see what all the noise was about, fell over him and landed in Mamma's lap.

"Oh my goodness," cried Mamma, "this is too much! You kittens are going to have to learn to be quieter and more gentle. I can't put up with this!"

The little kittens were not used to seeing Mamma so upset. They hurried to clean up the mess. Meanwhile, Mamma had been thinking.

"My cousin Mildred has just had some new kittens," she said. "I'll ask her to stay. Then you will have to be quiet and careful."

Cousin Mildred's new kittens were tiny! At first the older kittens were afraid to touch them, but they soon found how nice it was to cuddle a little furry bundle.

Later, as the little kittens took turns holding the babies, Tiger Tail had a good idea.

"Can't we have some little brothers and sisters, Mamma?" he asked.

Mamma Father Cat exchanged a smile. "We'll see," they said.

The Mighty Mouse

One morning at school, Mrs. Mumbles told the little kittens all about mice. Now kittens and cats are very interested in mice, as you can imagine, but these days, with good home cooking and lots of stores where cats can buy food, many younger kittens have never come face to face with a real live mouse.

In the playground after the lesson, Bella was pretending to know everything as usual.

"Ordinary mice are no problem," she said. "What you need to worry about are giant mice. They are twice as big as a grown-up cat and twice as fierce."

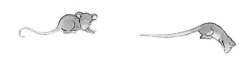

The little kittens were impressed by this. They tried to imagine what a giant mouse might look like, but since they had never seen even an ordinary mouse, that was difficult.

That evening, Rolypoly tossed and turned in his bed. Every time he closed his eyes, he seemed to see the staring eyes of a monster that just might be a giant mouse. At last, unable to sleep, he crept out of bed and tiptoed toward the kitchen.

Just then, he happened to glance over his shoulder.

"Aaaaaah!" he squeaked. There on the wall was a giant shadow. It had whiskers! It had a tail! It was a giant mouse!

Mamma Cat soon made Rolypoly feel better. Can you guess what she told him?

Five More Minutes

Mamma Cat put down her knitting. "Time for bed, kittens," she said.

But all the little kittens cried out, "Oh no, Mamma, just five more minutes, please!"

Mamma looked at her kittens. Two of them were painting pictures, one was reading a book, and the other two were playing a quiet game of tiddlywinks.

"All right," she said. "Just five more minutes. Then it is definitely bedtime."

She looked up at the clock as she spoke and noticed that it said seven thirty. Mamma sighed and sipped her cocoa. Maybe it was the cocoa, or maybe it was just because Mamma was so tired these days, but before long the kittens noticed that she had fallen asleep.

Quick as a flash, and as quietly as his paws would carry him, Tiger Tail crept over to the clock. He stopped the hands at seven thirty!

When Mamma Cat woke up, she looked at the clock. She knew she'd been asleep, but it looked as if no time had passed at all. Just a minute! Wasn't that a painty pawmark on the clock?

Mamma smiled. "There's some milk in the kitchen," she said. "Run along and drink it."

The kittens ran out of the room. Quick as a flash, Mamma ran over to the clock and moved the hands forward.

As five pairs of milky whiskers returned, she called out, "Bedtime now, kittens! It's half past midnight!"

The little kittens knew that Mamma had played a trick on them, but they couldn't say anything without admitting they had tried it, too!

The Biggest Balloon

The five little kittens were very excited. They were getting ready for their birthday party.

"Quiet, please!" called Mamma, who was busy trying to decorate five special birthday cakes to please her five kittens. "Why don't you all take a break from what you're doing and blow up balloons together?"

And that is just what the kittens did.

232

"My balloons are the biggest!" called Tiger Tail. "This one is huge!"

Rolypoly looked at his brother's balloon.

"This one is big … *puff!*" he gasped, and took a deep breath. "It's bigger than Mopsy's … *puff!* … It's bigger than Fluffy's … *puff!* … It's bigger than Honeybun's … *puff!* … It's even … bigger … than … *puff!* …Tiger Tail's! Just …" Before Rolypoly could finish his sentence, there was a loud *POP!*

Kittens always make a wish when a balloon goes pop.

"I wished for roller skates," said Rolypoly.

"I wished for a nurse's kit," said Fluffy.

"I wished for a book," said Mopsy.

"I wished for a ball," said Honeybun.

"I wished for a baby brother," said Tiger Tail.

Mamma Cat laughed, thinking about the presents already wrapped up and hidden carefully under her bed.

"Well, maybe your wishes will come true," she said.

The Cat in the Moon

One spring evening, Father Cat took all the little kittens outside to look at the stars. And there was the cat in the moon as well.

But Tiger Tail hung his head.

"I can't see it," he said sadly.

Patiently, Father Cat tried to show Tiger Tail where the cat was, but Tiger Tail made an excuse and went inside.

"I'm going to take you to have your eyes tested," said Mamma Cat. "It won't hurt a bit, and you might be able to see better afterwards."

Mr. Specks the eye doctor looked carefully at Tiger Tail's eyes and asked him to read some letters on a chart.

"Well, young kitten," he said, "you need a pair of glasses."

The following week, Mamma and Tiger Tail went to pick up the glasses.

Tiger Tail wrinkled up his nose and refused to open his eyes as Mr. Specks fitted them. Then he took just a little peek, and cried out.

"I can see a bee on the window! I can see a penny on the floor! Oh, and when I look in the mirror, I can see me!"

Tiger Tail was so pleased with his bright new world that he didn't give another thought to the glasses on his nose.

That night, he too saw the cat in the moon. "My glasses are so good that I can see him waving to me!" he laughed.

The Quacking Kitten

Farmer Feather met Father Cat in the lane.

"How are things with you and your family?" asked Farmer Feather.

"As chaotic as usual," smiled Father Cat. "How are things on the farm?"

"Oh, I love this time of year," smiled Farmer Feather. "There is always so much going on in the spring, with new little ones popping up all over the place."

"Yes, indeed," smiled Father Cat.

"Perhaps your little kittens would like to come down to the barnyard," said the kind farmer. "There are lots of little chicks and ducklings hatching out just now. But you will warn them to be quiet, won't you?"

"Well, I'll try," said Father Cat doubtfully.

As soon as they reached the farmyard, the kittens could see that it was full of hurrying and scurrying and a sense of excitement.

"Oh, look!" cried Tiger Tail. Down by the pond, a mother duck was standing over her nest. In front of her were three eggs—and there were cracks in them! Tiger Tail watched in wonder as first one, then two, then three little heads popped out of the eggs.

As they shook their feathers in the sunshine, the three ducklings looked around. And the first thing they saw was Tiger Tail.

With a squawk, the ducklings waddled off their nest and looked up at Tiger Tail. They thought he was their mother!

"I see my hens and ducks are not the only ones to get new families," laughed Farmer Feather. "Tiger Tail, they think you're … *quackers!*"

First Day of School

Mrs. Mumbles had an announcement for the kittens one day.

"We have two new kittens joining us this morning. Here are Daisy and Maisy," she said. "Or is it Maisy and Daisy?"

The new kittens were twins! Fluffy looked as closely as she could without being rude, but she simply could not tell them apart.

As the morning wore on, it became obvious that no one else could either, including Mrs. Mumbles. The new kittens were grinning.

At lunchtime, the kittens lined up to be given milk by Mrs. Mumbles.

"Just a minute … er … Maisy," said the teacher, "I've already given you your milk, haven't I?"

"No, Mrs. Mumbles, that was Daisy," said the kitten, looking as sweet as blueberry pie.

But five minutes later, Mrs. Mumbles found herself giving a very similar kitten another glass of milk.

"It is easy to get confused, isn't it?" smiled the twin. "I'm afraid you must have given my sister two glasses!"

By the end of the day, Mrs. Mumbles' patience was running out.

"You will have to wear something that will help me tell you apart," she said.

So the kittens wore two little chains, one with an M and one with a D. Mrs. Mumbles was very relieved. It was a good thing she didn't see those kittens deciding which to wear each morning!

239

Kittens to Cuddle

One fine day, Doctor Duckweed came to the little kittens' home. He had a few quiet words with Mamma Cat, rescued his stethoscope from Rolypoly, who was seeing if he could ping balls of paper with it, and waved merrily as he went off down the path.

"Goodbye, Mrs. Cat," he called. "It won't be long now!"

That night, Mamma Cat told the kittens to go to bed earlier than usual.

"But why, Mamma?" asked Mopsy. "I haven't finished my book."

But just then, Tiger Tail, who was looking into a basket Mamma kept behind her chair, said, "Ooooh!" and "Yes, we'll go to bed now!"

Mamma gave Tiger Tail a secret smile, and Tiger Tail immediately took charge.

Tiger Tail was the first little kitten to get up the next morning, but the others were not far behind. Following Tiger Tail, they crept into Mamma's room. She was sitting up in bed with a big smile on her face—and three baby kittens in her arms!

Before long, the five big kittens were snuggling on the bed with their baby brother and sisters.

"They're so sweet," said Father Cat proudly. "We love them to bits."

Tiger Tail whispered in Mamma's ear.

"You do still love us too, don't you?"

"More than ever, sweetheart," smiled Mamma. "More than ever."

Bedtime Tales

Time For Bed!

Choose your sleepytime story from this
cuddly and comical collection.

Fred-Under-the-Bed

It was time for Jake and Rosie to go to bed.

"But there's a Fred under my bed!" cried Jake.

"What do you mean?" asked his mother.

"It's what happens to socks," said Jake. "They turn into sock monsters. Ours is called Fred."

"Goodnight!" laughed his mother.

Jake and Rosie jumped into bed, but right away a funny little figure crawled out from under Jake's bed. It was certainly Fred.

"If you're looking for socks again, you can't have any. We're fed up with finding only odd socks to wear," said Jake.

"But I'm hungry," said the sock monster. "Isn't there anything else? I could manage a glove or a pair of mittens."

"We need those," said Rosie.

"If I don't have something soon," said the sock monster, "I'm going to start munching your teddy bears."

"This calls for action!" whispered Jake. "You give him my scarf to nibble. I'll grab him!"

"Fnnfnfn!" shouted the sock monster, as Jake ran off with him and threw him into the washing machine.

Next morning, when the twins saw the laundry flapping on the line, they felt sure that the sock monster was gone for ever. What do you think?

The Magic Quilt

Once upon a time, there was a woman who loved to sew. She made beautiful dresses for her daughters and fine suits for her sons. But the years passed. One by one, her children left home and settled in faraway lands. From time to time, they sent letters home to their mother, but in all her busy life, she had never learned to read. She kept the letters in a chest, tied up with ribbons, until a friend from the nearby town could come to tell her what they said.

As the woman grew older, she could no longer work. At last, she became too weak to look after herself. Her friend invited her to stay. All she took with her was the chest from the foot of her bed.

"If only you could read," said her friend, "it would give you something to do all day."

Next morning, the woman suddenly knew what she must do. She asked her friend to open up her old chest and put it within her reach. Inside, as well as the letters from her children, there were all the scraps of fabric left over from her sewing over the years. Slowly, with stiff fingers, she sewed them together.

The beautiful quilt covered the old woman's bed from top to toe. In her mind she journeyed to far off places, thinking of memories held by each piece of fabric.

"This is a book that I *can* read," she smiled.

A Bear With No Name

When a bear has found a good home, with children who love him, there is only one more thing he needs: a name. And that is why, when the bear in this story had been in his new home for over a month and still hadn't been given a name, he began to feel very concerned.

As a matter of fact, it wasn't very strange at all, for the little boy he now belonged to was only ten days old! The little boy was called Jack. He could sleep, and he could cry, and he could drink his milk, but he couldn't talk.

Time passed. Soon Jack could sit up and put his arms around the bear.

"When he can talk," thought the bear, "Jack will give me a name. I know he will."

But things did not turn out as the bear expected. One morning, the little boy sat up in his bed and stretched out his arms. "Bear!" he said. "Bear! Bear!" It was his very first word.

Then, one day, Jack had a new baby sister. Her aunt gave her a bear of her own, and from the start everyone called the new bear Honey.

"And what is your name?" Honey asked Jack's bear, when he introduced himself.

"He calls me Bear," replied the bear, waiting for Honey to laugh.

But Honey didn't laugh. "Oh, you are lucky," she said. "What a distinguished name. Only the very finest bear could possibly be called Bear!"

That night, when Jack snuggled down in bed with his bear, he whispered, "Goodnight, Bear!" as he always did. And Bear could hardly sleep because he was bursting with pride.

"Goodnight, Boy!" he whispered back.

Oh No, Not Again!

There was once a little elf called Juniper Jingle who lived in a tree trunk with his mother and his granny.

But Juniper's mother and granny found him very hard to live with. You see, Juniper had wonderful dreams, but they always had the same result. Juniper tossed and turned so much in his sleep that he fell out of bed. And when Juniper fell with a thud, the whole tree shook and everyone woke up, except Juniper Jingle, who slept on as if nothing had happened … on the floor.

Mrs. Jingle had tried everything to keep Juniper in his bed. Finally, she decided she must go to see the Fidget Fairy for a magic spell. The Fidget Fairy knew at once what to do. "Juniper is a most extraordinary elf," she said. "An imagination like that should be encouraged. I will give you a spell to make him an imaginary bed, and everything will be well."

Mrs. Jingle was not convinced, but when she got home she said the spell exactly as she had been taught it. At once, Juniper's old bed disappeared … and nothing came in its place. Mrs. Jingle was just about to go back to the fairy to complain when Juniper walked in.

"Wow!" he said. "Wow and double wow! That's a wonderful bed!" And he climbed up into mid-air and lay there, as comfortable as could be.

Juniper still has wonderful dreams, but no matter how much he tosses and turns, he never hits the floor. And everyone else is happy, too.

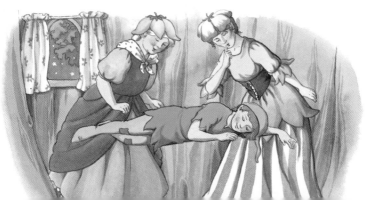

Aunt Aggie Comes to Stay

The very first time Aunt Aggie came to stay with Louisa and her family, they didn't guess that she would bring so much with her! This is what she brought: a huge trunk; one pink, one orange, one yellow, one blue, and one brown case; a picnic hamper that was extraordinarily heavy; a guitar in a case; a striped bicycle; several large bags; a parrot in a cage; and an enormous bunch of flowers!

Aunt Aggie had wonderful stories to tell. Louisa loved having her to stay.

At last the day came when it was time for Aunt Aggie to go home. Into her truck went a huge trunk, one pink, one orange, one yellow, one blue, and one brown case, a picnic hamper, a guitar in a case, a striped bicycle, several large bags, a parrot in a cage, a huge box that had once contained a dishwasher, and Aunt Aggie.

"Goodbye!" she called. "See you next year!"

It wasn't until ten minutes later that someone said, "Where's Louisa?" and someone else said, "What was in that dishwasher box?"

An anxious five minutes passed, and Aunt Aggie's truck came squealing up to the door.

"Next year," said Louisa's dad later, "we'll check everything in the truck before she drives away."

Louisa smiled. She had a whole year to think of a plan!

The Babyish Bear

When Jack was given a big present for his birthday, he was impressed. It was from Mrs. Marino, an elderly lady who lived nearby.

As soon as he had ripped off the paper, Jack changed his mind. It was a great big fluffy teddy bear with a ribbon around his neck. Even Jack's mother hid a smile.

"How lovely, sweetheart," she said. "You must say thank you to Mrs. Marino when you see her."

Jack's mind was already on other problems. The bear had to be hidden—and fast. His friends were coming to his party in a couple of hours, and there was no way they could see this bear. If only it wasn't so enormous—there simply seemed nowhere to hide it.

It was almost time for the party when Jack had a brilliant idea.

"If I hurry, I've just got time to go and thank Mrs. Marino," he told his mother.

When Mrs. Marino opened the door, his words came out in a rush. "Mrs.-Marino-thank-you-very-much-for-my-present-but-it's-my-party-and-I'm-afraid-he-might-get-damaged-so-could-you-keep-him-for-me-this-afternoon-please?"

Mrs. Marino looked puzzled. "Well, you won't want a bear at your age, will you? Did you like the watch?"

Then Mrs. Marino showed him the opening in the bear's back where you could tuck things away and explained that she thought the bear would stop it getting squashed or stood on among all his presents.

"Old people," Jack told his mother later, "are strange, but they're okay too. Oh look, it's *time* for my party!"

Rainbow Ribbons

When an elf goes courting, he always takes the lady of his choice some ribbons for her hair. Elderflower Elf went shopping one day for ribbons to take to Emmeline. He stood for some time in the shop full of ribbons and laces.

In the end, he chose green ones, to match dear Emmeline's eyes. Then he wandered home, thinking of those eyes, and fell into a ditch as a result, annoying a frog who lived there.

Unfortunately, Emmeline's beautiful eyes lit up for only a moment when she saw the ribbons.

"I was hoping you would bring orange ones," Emmeline sighed.

But the elf was already running back to the shop as fast as he could— and colliding with that frog again.

Emmeline considered the new orange ribbons for a second—before expressing a preference for blue.

Back went Elderflower. *Splash!* You guessed it. The frog wasn't happy.

Back at her rose bower, Emmeline sighed. Somehow there was something about Elderflower that just didn't appeal to her. She was about to send him off for violet ribbons, just to get rid of him, when…

"I wonder if these are to your taste, my dear?" said a deep voice, and a jumping gentleman in green offered her a bow of beautiful rainbow ribbons.

Emmeline married her frog and lived happily ever after. And Elderflower set up his own shop in an oak tree to sell ribbons to other elves!

A Puppet For Polly

For her fourth birthday, Polly asked for a puppet. She didn't ask nicely. She didn't say "please". She said, "I want a puppet!" very loudly. That was the kind of little girl Polly Chin was.

Polly's dad was firm. She couldn't have everything she wanted, he said. But Polly's Aunt Naomi just smiled. On the little girl's birthday morning, there was a package from Aunt Naomi and inside was a big, beautiful, clown puppet. Polly ignored all her other presents and started playing with it at once.

"Time for swimming!" called her dad a little later. "Get your things, sweetheart."

"No!" said Polly. "Come with me, Mr. Clown. We'll hide upstairs."

"No!" said the puppet.

Polly was so surprised, she dropped him! "Ow!" cried Mr. Clown. "Don't treat me like that!"

"I'm sorry," said the little girl, which was not something she often said.

That night, Polly played with her puppet again. But Dad was already calling up the stairs. "Time for bed, birthday girl!"

"Not yet!" shouted Polly.

"No way!" said the puppet. Once again, Polly looked in disbelief. "I mean," Mr. Clown went on, "we haven't finished playing yet. That man is rude and mean."

It didn't take Polly long to realize that when she was naughty, Mr. Clown was naughty too. And when she was good… well, you can imagine. Her dad noticed the difference.

"You know," he told his older sister Naomi, "ever since she's had that clown, she's been a nicer child. What a relief!"

Naomi smiled. "I remember," she said, "how it worked with a naughty little boy I grew up with."

But Polly's dad, like Polly sometimes, pretended not to hear!

Why Am I Blue?

Once upon a time, there was an elephant called Little Blue.

He lived with his family on a dusty plain, munching and marching, marching and munching. One day, the elephants came to a waterhole that was not as muddy as usual. It had clear, clean water, sparkling in the sunshine.

Mother Elephant ushered Little Blue to the front. She didn't want him to be left behind. The little elephant looked down. Another little elephant looked back at him. It was the first time that Little Blue had seen his reflection. It was wonderful!

It was only when he was full of the clear, clean water that the little elephant turned to his mother and asked, "Why am I blue?" He could see now that none of the other elephants looked at all like him.

"You are blue because blue is right for you," Little Blue's mother replied.

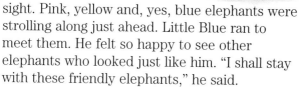

But Little Blue felt strange and different. Then, one day, far away across the plain, he saw a wonderful sight. Pink, yellow and, yes, blue elephants were strolling along just ahead. Little Blue ran to meet them. He felt so happy to see other elephants who looked just like him. "I shall stay with these friendly elephants," he said.

But that night, as he tried to sleep under the stars, Little Blue realized he didn't really belong with the strange elephants. Under the huge moon, he trotted back to his own family.

"I'm so glad you're back, Little Blue," whispered his mother. "So am I," said Little Blue.

263

Are You There, Mr. Bear?

All day long, strange noises came from Mr. Bear's house. There was clattering and banging and, I'm sorry to say, some angry words, too. Everyone wondered what Mr. Bear could possibly be doing.

By the end of the afternoon, a small crowd had gathered outside Mr. Bear's house. Still the strange noises went on.

"He wouldn't hear even if we did knock and offer to help," said a panda, which made everyone feel much better.

As the moon rose in the sky, the animals went back to their own homes. Gradually the noises from Mr. Bear's house stopped and only Mr. Bear's snoring could be heard.

The next morning, Mr. Bear strolled down the street, greeting everyone he met with a friendly word and a wave. It was a long time since he had done *that*!

Mrs. Rabbit went to find out what had happened. "I met Mr. Bear in the lane," she told her husband later, "and soon found out all about it. He's been bad tempered because he hasn't been getting a wink of sleep. Some birds built their nest under the eaves and kept him awake with their twittering. All day yesterday he was hauling his bed downstairs. He's just had his first full night's sleep in weeks."

"But it won't last long," Mrs. Rabbit said. "A family of mice has just moved in under the floorboards!"

All at Sea

Petunia Panda was reading a bedtime book to her little ones. It was a rhyme about an owl and a pussy-cat who sailed away in a beautiful pea-green boat. All the baby pandas loved it, especially Patrick. His head was so full of sailing and bong-trees and piggywigs that he began to dream about them as soon as his head touched the pillow. But Patrick's dream started to go wrong from the very beginning.

Patrick's boat wasn't pea-green. It was red. And instead of a pussy-cat there was a kangaroo!

"Please don't bounce!" cried Patrick. "Oh! Please don't bounce!"

"Of course not," said the kangaroo. But the next moment, Patrick found himself in the wettest water he had ever known. He swam to the upturned boat, which drifted toward an island.

At last the boat landed with a bump on the sandy shore of the island. Patrick wondered what would happen next. And just then, a coconut tumbled down and bounced off his head.

"Ouch!" To Patrick's amazement, he wasn't asleep any longer, but his little brother Peter was banging him on the head with his toy kangaroo.

"I'm glad you've woken up at last," announced Peter.

"So am I," said Patrick. "So am I!"

The Rainy Day

Mrs. Millie Mouse looked out of the window at the rain. "Poor Daphne!" she sighed. Mr. Mouse knew exactly what she meant. His wife's sister Daphne was getting married and he had heard of little else for weeks.

Mrs. Mouse put on her raincoat and hat and hurried out into the rain. She needed to visit her friends to discuss what to do with the mountains of food they had all been preparing. And what about the amazingly huge hats they had all made, each trying to outdo the other?

Mrs. Mouse found all her friends at Mrs. Martha Mouse's large house.

"I'd love to offer to have the wedding here," cried Mrs. Martha Mouse, "but there isn't room for three hundred and fifty guests."

"Underground, maybe?" queried Millie Mouse.

"Oh no! It would be so dark and cramped. And my hat won't fit in the passages!"

Now you may notice that we have not yet met Daphne and her fiancé Tom. As a matter of fact, neither of them wanted all this fuss, which had been arranged entirely by the mouse ladies without consulting them at all.

At that moment, the two mice in question were making sure their dream of a quiet wedding came true.

"I love the rain," sighed Daphne. "Don't you?"

"Almost as much," smiled Tom, "as I love you."

Trouble in the Toy Box

When Leila went to bed at the end of a long and exciting day, she fell asleep almost at once. It was her birthday. She had received lots of wonderful presents and enjoyed her party.

While Leila slept peacefully in her bed, there was a terrible groaning and sighing from her toy box. It was a special box, shaped like a pirate's chest, that her uncle had given her last year for her birthday.

"That panda is sitting on my elbow!" said a grumpy voice.

"You'd feel worse if you had a train standing on your toes," moaned another voice.

"We were fine in here," said the ragdoll firmly, "until all these new toys arrived today. They should go."

"Did you see how happy Leila was when she saw us?" asked a yo-yo. "The old toys must go."

All night long, the toys pushed and shoved each other, until half of them fell on the floor.

270

Next morning, Leila's uncle arrived. "I'm sorry I couldn't make it yesterday," he said, "but I've brought your present today."

"Oh no!" Leila's dad groaned. "We've got trouble finding room for the toys we've got already."

But Leila's uncle just grinned. "Then it's a good thing I couldn't think of a different present this year," he said. And he carried in … another enormous toy box!

What's That?

One night, Baby Bear woke up feeling hungry. He knew that there was some apple pie in the kitchen, so he scrambled out of bed.

In his bedroom, the moonlight made it easy to see where he was going. But outside in the hallway it was very dark. Baby Bear set off along the carpet, feeling in front of him with his paws at every step. When he couldn't feel anything at all in front of him, he knew he had reached the stairs and crept down them.

"Not far to that pie now," said Baby Bear to himself. But just then, he heard a noise.

"What's that?" The little bear was worried.

As he turned toward the kitchen, he heard another sound.

"What's that?" he wondered.

Baby Bear put his hand on the kitchen doorknob. He opened the door rapidly to get the squeaking over as quickly as possible and…

"What's that?" cried a deep voice.

"What's that?" squeaked Baby Bear.

He found himself face to tummy with Papa Bear … and Papa Bear was holding a large slice of apple pie!

The two bears looked at each other for a long minute.

Then, "Sshh!" said Papa Bear. "We must munch very, very quietly."

And they did.

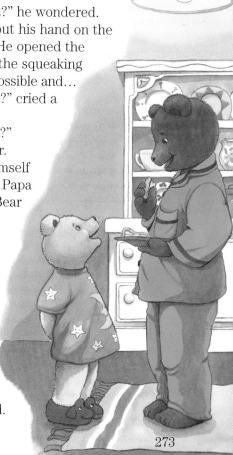

273

Birthday Books

Grown-up people can be very bad at remembering things. So how is it they (usually) remember your birthday? That's the work of the birthday fairy, who whispers in their ears a week or so before each important day.

The fairies have special books, where all the birthdays in the world are written down. They are all kept in the Lilac Library. A very old elf has been the librarian for years and years. He is helped by a team of lively little elves.

One day, there was a terrible commotion in the Lilac Library. A book had gone missing! It was the one for October 17th, Volume 96.

The elves searched all day, looking everywhere in the library.

The fairy concerned was beside herself with anxiety.

"Don't worry, my dear," cried the Chief Librarian. "Come back in half an hour and I'll have a list of names for you."

As soon as the fairy had gone, the old elf pressed a secret button under his desk. A whole shelf of books swung open, and the Librarian slipped inside to his secret room. There was a computer with a smile on its screen.

"Can I help you?" it asked.

In no time at all, a long list of all the birthdays for October 17th curled out of the machine.

The fairy was delighted with the list and promised not to tell about the back-up system. And the Librarian soon found he had been sitting on the missing volume all the time!

The Tumbling Clown

T here was complete silence in the toyshop. Everyone looked in horror at the tumbling clown, who stood proudly in his yellow and blue costume on the highest shelf.

"I can't bear to look!" whispered the little blue rabbit.

The tumbling clown put his nose in the air. "None of you has any idea of my abilities," he said. "I was made to tumble and tumble I will! Can I have a long drumroll, please, Pink Teddy Bear?"

Drrr! Drrr! Drrr!

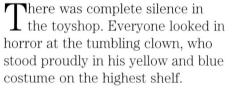

The clown
raised his hands in the air.

He jumped off the shelf…
making a somersault…

a double back flip…
touched his toes…

and landed on
the back of one of the
elephants belonging
to the toy Noah's ark.

"Wow! That was great!" cried
the jumping frog. "Will you show me
how you did it?"

The next day, all the toys had
lessons in acrobatics. Even the little
blue rabbit could do a double-eared
spin with tail twist.

So, if you have a little brother
or sister whose toys are always flying
out of the bed, you'll know it's not the
baby's fault at all. Those toys have
been taught by the tumbling clown,
and they won't stay still no matter
what you do!

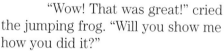

A Bear at Bathtime

Johanna wanted to take her bear everywhere, but her mother was firm.

"Sweetheart, he can't go in the bathtub," she would say. "He'll get soaking and soggy. You won't be able to take him to bed with you."

But Johanna didn't want to listen. Each night at bathtime there were loud words from Johanna, and there were firm words from her mother. There was not very much at all from her teddy bear, who was forced to sit on a shelf until Johanna was dry and ready for bed.

One day, Johanna's Aunt May came to babysit. Aunt May knew, of course, that bears don't go in bathtubs, but she didn't

know she had to watch young Johanna every second of bathtime. In went the bear, hidden by the bubbles. It wasn't until Johanna dragged the soaking, furry toy out of the bathtub that Aunt May realized what she had done.

"You can't take a wet bear to bed with you, and that's final," she told the little girl. When Johanna went to sleep at last, Aunt May took the bear down to the drier and put him in.

Next morning, Johanna's mother looked curiously at Johanna and her bear.

"Your bear looks smaller," she said.

"He isn't smaller," said Johanna quickly (although he was). "It's just that I've grown!"

279

No More Cake!

When Agatha Mouse hopped on the scales in the bathroom one morning, she let out a little shriek of alarm. All the little mice jumped.

"Oh no," groaned Ethel. "It's no-more-cake time."

"It certainly is," sighed their mother. "I'm afraid it's no-more-cake-for-a-long time."

The little mice sighed, too. They knew what their mother was like during no-more-cake times. She was miserable. She was grumpy. But worst of all, she stopped baking. She didn't make

280

pies. She didn't make puddings. And, of course, she didn't make cakes! She usually decided she needed more exercise, too, so she walked to school to collect the little mice each day.

Agatha Mouse's no-more-cake times could sometimes last for weeks. The little mice gritted their teeth and tried not to think about muffins and pies. You can imagine how surprised they were when, only two days later, they found Mrs. Mouse baking and singing in the kitchen.

"My dears," smiled Agatha. "It's no-more-being-naughty-little-mice time. It's can-we-do-anything-to-help-you-dear-mother time. We're going to have some babies! That's why the scales said I was heavier. Now get ready for bed. And make the most of it! Soon it's going to be waking-up-in-the-middle-of-the-night time!"

The Sniffles

Bobby Bunny was getting ready to go out to play when his mother called him back.

"You need your scarf on a day like this," she said. "We don't want you catching the sniffles, do we?"

Bobby was puzzled. "How do Sniffles look?" he asked.

"Droopy ears, a red nose, and wiggly whiskers," grunted his father.

Bobby ran out to play with his friends. He had a wonderful time. The sun was already beginning to go down when he set off for home.

The trees made dark shadows on the lane as Bobby scuttled along. He suddenly began to think about the Sniffles. More than once he turned his head to make sure there wasn't a Sniffles creeping along behind him.

Just then, there was a swooshing noise in a nearby field.

Bobby gulped. He parted the branches and
peered through the bushes. There in
the field was a huge creature. It had
floppy ears, a red nose, and … yes …
wiggly whiskers. It was a Sniffles!
Bobby ran home as fast as he could.

When Bobby told his
story to his family, Father
Bunny set out to find the
Sniffles. It turned out to
be an old scarecrow!
Father told Bobby
what the sniffles
really were.

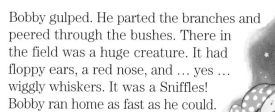

"I've learned something tonight," smiled
Bobby. "It's not catching the sniffles you have to
worry about, it's the sniffles catching you!"

The Balloon Bear

When a cross little girl called Emily went to the fair with her grandma, she was very hard to please. She didn't enjoy anything. Then Emily spotted a man selling balloons of every size and shape. "I want one of those," she said.

Grandma let Emily choose a balloon shaped like a bear. Emily didn't say thank you. She just marched off toward the gates and home. But a lady coming the other way bumped into her. It was only a little bump, but Emily let go of her balloon. The bear went floating up into the air.

"I want to go home," said Emily. "I've had a horrible time."

What Emily and her grandma didn't notice was that the balloon bear was bobbing along above them.

"How was the fair?" Emily's mother asked at the garden gate.

"Boring," said Emily.

"And the rides?"

"Boring."

At that moment, the balloon bear floated gently down until it settled on the roses. POP! went the balloon bear just behind Emily, who sat down with a bump and a very surprised expression on her face.

"Well, there was one bit that I enjoyed," said Grandma, and even Emily laughed.

285

One by One

Mr. Noah studied his charts. "I've built it exactly as I was told," he said to his wife, "but still, it doesn't look right somehow."

"The ark is fine," said Mrs. Noah. "It's just the door that looks out of proportion. Are you sure you got the measurements right?"

"I've checked and checked," replied her husband. "It's high time we started loading the animals. I don't like the look of those clouds."

Dutifully, the animals lined up. Two by two, up the plank, trotted the flamingos and the porcupines. Two by two came the hippos. Ooops! There was no doubt about it, two hippos side by side would not fit through the door.

"I knew it!" cried Mr. Noah. "I'm afraid you'll just have to go in one by one."

One by one went the reindeer. One by one went the zebras. Ooops! Even one elephant just would not fit through the door.

"That settles it!" said Mr. Noah. "I simply must have made a mistake about the door."

Mr. Noah set to work to make a much larger doorway. After that, there was no trouble loading the animals, but one creature was missing.

"Mrs. Flea, come along!" called Mr. Noah.

A tiny speck hopped off his chart. Mr. Noah peered at the paper. "Bless my soul, what a difference a zero makes," he said. "No wonder the measurements were wrong!"

Clip, Clip, Clop!

Dusty the horse leaned over the gate. "What are you doing, Percy?" he asked.

"Sssssh!" said Percy Pig. "Don't interrupt me, old friend. I'm reading my book."

Dusty blew through his nose rudely. "I don't know why you want to do that," he said.

"You don't like reading because you're not very good at it, Dusty," said Percy. "And that's because you don't do it enough."

Dusty kicked up his heels and snorted again. "It still seems boring to me," he said, "and books are always about silly things anyway."

"Well, that's where you're wrong, old friend," replied Percy. "This book happens to be about a horse, and it's very interesting."

Dusty was not in a very good mood by the time Percy joined him. He was sulking and sighing as the two of them set off down the road.

"Just a minute, Dusty," puffed Percy, "there's something I need to talk to you about."

"Well?" said Dusty shortly.

"It's just that in my book," said Percy, ignoring the snort this brought from his friend, "the horse went *clip, clop, clip, clop* down the lane. But I couldn't help noticing that you're going *clip, clip, clop, clop*."

Dusty looked down at his hooves. One of his shoes was very loose and he'd been sulking too much to notice.

A quick trip to the blacksmith soon fixed Dusty's problem. Nowadays, Dusty has a new respect for books— especially ones about horses and pigs!

Be Brave, Lian!

Lian was afraid of dragons. She lived in a country where the storybooks were full of dragons. She never went anywhere without a big silk bag containing her secret anti-dragon kit. I don't know what was in it, but even Lian didn't put all her faith in it. Her real plan, when the dreadful day arrived, was to run.

One day, she set off for her grandma's house, which was over the hill and through the woods. Lian reached the top of the hill and set off down the other side. Far below among the trees, there was a great big puff of smoke. Then another one.

There was absolutely no doubt in Lian's mind. There was an enormous dragon down there!

Lian was frightened of dragons, but she loved her grandma very much. She set off down the hill toward the smoke, clutching her anti-dragon kit, to rescue the old lady.

The dragon was making a dreadful noise, roaring and panting down in the valley. Lian ran faster. When she reached her grandma's house, she rushed in without knocking.

"Ah, here you are!" said Grandma. "Isn't this exciting?" She grabbed Lian's hand and dragged her out of the house. The panting and roaring got louder as Grandma hurried along, and when Lian looked up, she found that the dragon's smokey breath was all around.

"There it is!" cried Grandma. "It's called a train!" Lian was never frightened of dragons again.

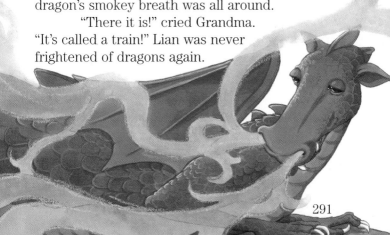

291

Don't Look Behind You!

Fred Rabbit was tired of taking his cousin Nibbles to school. Nibbles was a whining, frightened young rabbit, who imagined foxes behind every bush and owls on every gate post. One evening, on the way home from school, he decided to teach Nibbles a lesson.

Just as the two rabbits were passing the spooky oak tree at the corner of the lane, Fred hissed, "Don't look behind you, Nibbles!"

"W-w-why not?" stuttered Nibbles.

"Because I think we're being followed by a Hoojymop," said Fred, "and you don't want to meet a Hoojymop on a Monday."

"W-w-why not?" asked Nibbles.

"Hoojymops are cuddly, friendly creatures all the rest of the week," said Nibbles, "but on Monday nights, they have to eat rabbit pie. It's the Hoojymop law."

Nibbles was very scared, but at last the two bunnies reached home. It was then that Nibbles remembered it was Tuesday!

Fred laughed. "Nothing will eat us today or any day if you use your head, Nibbles," he said, "like you're using it now. If you think about what frightens you, you can make it go away. Even a Hoojymop!" And he was right, you know!

Doctor Do-A-Lot

When Doctor Do-A-Lot came calling, he rushed upstairs to the patient and dashed back down again before you could say, "Good morning, Doctor!" In fact, before you said "Good..." he thrust a piece of paper into your hand and whirled away, waving his top hat.

The piece of paper was one of Doctor Do-A-Lot's famous prescriptions. Some of them were the kind of thing you would expect. Others were a little stranger. To Lazy Leonard he prescribed helping Mrs. Marvel with the laundry for her twelve children. For Miss Paddle's moping, he prescribed trombone lessons!

Everyone in Elftown loved Doctor Do-A-Lot, so they were very upset when they heard that the doctor himself was not feeling well. But when they asked if he had toothache, or tummy ache, or fidgety feet, he said no.

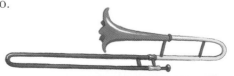

The elves were worried. What would happen to Doctor Do-A-Lot? And what would happen to them when they were ill if he could not look after them? But when old Mrs. Mapleleaf heard about the problem, she let out a cackle and scribbled on a piece of paper.

"Take this to Doctor Do-A-Lot," she said. "He'll soon get better."

And when the doctor saw the paper, he burst into laughter and shooed everyone out of his house.

"I need to get some rest," he said. "I'll see you all next week."

And the paper? Doctor Do-A-Lot framed it and put it on his wall. It said:

Take 12 hours of rest and proper meals plus a dash of common sense every single day!

Little Cousin Clare

When Bryn heard that his little cousin Clare was coming to visit, he was very excited. Straight away, he began to plan the games he would play with Clare.

Bryn got out all his trucks and cars and arranged them in a line. He decided Clare could choose first which to play with.

"I'm glad to see you're tidying up, Bryn," said Dad, when he came in from the fields. "Your playroom looks much better now."

But Bryn hadn't finished. He started to sort out his books and put all the ones about animals and all the ones about trucks together.

Last of all, Bryn organised his building bricks. It took ages.

The next day, Bryn waited for the sound of wheels in the driveway. When they came, he ran out with his mother.

"Bryn," she smiled, "I want to introduce you to your Aunt Jo."

Aunt Jo bent down. "And I want to introduce you to your cousin Clare," she said.

Bryn looked right into the face of a tiny, sleeping baby.

"Um… Excuse me," he said. "I just have to put some things away."

Bryn put away his toys and found his old blue bear instead. After all, there's nothing like a baby to make you feel much more grown-up than you've ever been before.

A Christmas Concert

As Christmas drew nearer, the little mice who lived among the roots of the oak tree became more and more excited. On the Friday before Christmas, Mrs. Mouse was taking them shopping at the edge of the forest. They couldn't wait.

But two weeks before Christmas, it began to snow. All week it snowed. On Thursday evening, Mrs. Mouse called the little mice to her and spoke seriously.

"I'm sorry, my dears," she said, "but the snow through the forest is so thick, we won't be able to visit the shops tomorrow."

The little mice looked at each other. What about the presents they had planned to buy?

"You are clever little mice," said Mrs.

Mouse. "I'm sure you could make your own presents if you tried hard."

The little mice were busy for days, but what could they make for Great Aunt Mouse, who already had everything she needed?

"She likes music," said one little mouse.

"She likes little mice," said another.

"We could put on a special Christmas Concert for her!" said a third.

And that is exactly what they did. It was a huge success. Every year since, the little mice have entertained all the grown-up mice from every part of the forest and back (if it's not snowing too hard)!

I Can't Fall Down!

The monkeys were chattering in the trees and bright sunlight was splashing the glossy leaves of the forest. Mrs. Parrot took her youngest son out on a branch and told him what he had to do.

"Just uncurl your feet and let go, Percy," she said. "Then flap your wings as hard as you can."

Percy peered through the leaves. "Mamma," he said, "I can't fall down!"

"It's not a question of falling down, Percy," said his mother sharply. "It's a question of flying. Your sisters can do it. Your brothers can do it. Every single one of your relatives can do it—except your little cousins and they're still in their eggs. Now, don't be a baby. Just let go."

But Percy simply wouldn't let go. When his mother gave him an encouraging nudge, he clung on tightly with his little feet. He wobbled. He wibbled. But he didn't let go. Mrs. Parrot sighed and left him to it.

"You were quite right," said a voice near Percy's ear. It was a young monkey. "It's much better not flying," said the new friend. "Follow me!" And the monkey strolled off along the branch. Percy followed hot on his heels. It was fine! No flying at all! Even when the monkey speeded up a bit, Percy still hopped along confidently. And when the monkey said, "Here you have to jump," Percy simply didn't think about it. He jumped.

Before he knew what was happening, Percy was flying!

Mrs. Parrot watched proudly. "Thanks, Mavis," she said to the monkey with a laugh.

By the Light of the Moon

Faraway on the top of the world, there is a place that is always cold, with white snow and icy sea. There are no trees and no flowers. There are only seals and fish and bears. And when those polar bears are about, the seals and fish need to watch out, because those bears can creep ever so quietly…

and slide ever so slippily…

and run ever so quickly…

and dive down into the deep blue sea with hardly a splash, when they are looking for a snack.

"I love being a polar bear!" one little bear told his mother once. "The sun shines all the time and makes the snow sparkle."

302

"Well, that is true," said his mother, "but you have not yet been alive for a whole year. In the summer the sun shines all the time, even at night. But in the winter, the sun doesn't shine at all. Not even in the daytime."

The little bear went away to think. The more he thought, the more he felt sad. The long, dark winter was coming, and it would be too dark to play and swim and slide.

One night, the little bear noticed that everything around him was deep blue and velvety.

"The sun has gone away until next year," said his mother. "It is winter now."

The little bear looked around. The snow was shining with a silvery light. It was the moon!

The little bear gave a sigh. There was nothing to fear. In the summer and the winter, he still lived in a wonderful world.

Ting-a-ling

Ting-a-ling was an elf with a problem. Everywhere he went, the bell on his hat went *ting-a-ling! ting-a-ling!* And the bell made things terribly difficult.

You see, Ting-a-ling was an artist. His special job was painting the wings of butterflies. The only way to paint them is to wait until they are sitting on a leaf and having a little snooze in the sun. You can guess what Ting-a-ling's problem was. He would lean back to take a look at his work and the bell on his hat would jingle.

In a flash, the butterfly would flap her wings and fly away. It was a disaster.

Ting-a-ling didn't know what to do. He couldn't take his hat off, because it was held on by magic. He was very unhappy.

One morning, Ting-a-ling started work on a butterfly

sitting right on the edge of a leaf. He had managed to finish one whole wing when his bell woke the butterfly. She flapped her wings together—and the wet paint on one wing made a pattern on the other wing that was just the same as the first!

After that, Ting-a-ling was a very happy elf. He always painted just one wing, yet all the butterflies looked beautiful. And his little bell was never a problem again.

You could try painting butterflies Ting-a-ling's way— but on paper, of course!

305

It's Too Quiet!

Mrs. Bear was having coffee with her friend Mrs. Katt. Their children were playing in the next room, but all of a sudden, Mrs. Katt looked up.

"It's too quiet in there," she said darkly.

Mrs. Bear and Mrs. Katt hurried to the door. The next room was deserted—but the window was wide open!

The two mothers tramped across the countryside, looking for their little ones. By the time they caught up with the runaways, they were hot and muddy and hungry.

306

That evening, Mrs. Bear was still cross when Mr. Bear came home from the forest. When he heard what had happened, he said, "Tomorrow, Karl Katt and I will look after the children, so that you and Karen Katt can have a day off. Those little ones really are a pawful these days."

Mrs. Bear agreed eagerly. The next morning, she sat with her friend once again, enjoying her coffee. Then she frowned.

"Are you thinking what I'm thinking?" she asked Mrs. Rabbit.

"I'm afraid so," said her friend. "I hate to say it, but I'll be glad when those little ones come home."

"It's just too quiet everywhere!" laughed the ladies.

The Perfect Present

Perhaps you have heard of Ellie Elf, who knows more magic than any elf in the seven kingdoms. Long ago, her grandmother taught her an important lesson. It was Ellie's birthday, and she had lots of presents, but she wondered what her grandmother would bring her.

It was late when Ellie's grandmother arrived

"It's a special day today, isn't it?" she said. "And I have something here for you. Hold out your hand."

But when Ellie looked down, all there was in her hand was a little pile of dusty seeds, some so tiny she could hardly see them.

"Plant them in the garden and see what happens," said her grandmother. "There's no need to look so disappointed, child!"

Reluctantly, Ellie planted her seeds. And she waited, but nothing happened. In the end, she forgot her seeds and didn't go near that corner of the garden for weeks.

One day, her grandmother came to visit again. "I've come to see your seeds," she smiled.

Ellie felt guilty. She thought there would be nothing to see. But the furthest corner of the garden was full of flowers!

It was magic!

Today, Ellie Elf is as wise as her grandmother once was. "The world is so magical," she says, "it hardly needs any help from me. Well, only a little bit…!"

The New Toys

Late one night, Daniel Harris's new toys decided to leave home. They had been looking at Daniel's books. The pictures of mountains and lakes and sailing ships were so exciting. They were amazed to find that somewhere there were castles and dragons and monsters.

"I want to visit the real sea," said the deep-sea diving doll.

"There are whole mountains for me to dig," said the yellow digger.

"And I'd like to run on some real rails," said the little red engine.

So that night, the toys crept out of the

310

house and into the garden. But those toys hadn't gone far before they stopped.

"The world is much, much bigger than I thought," said the diving doll.

"I could dig these flower beds for ever and ever and I still wouldn't finish," said the digger.

"And I'm beginning to think my little wheels wouldn't fit on great big tracks," sighed the engine. The toys decided to return home.

The next evening, Daniel's mother read him a story. The toys listened and smiled knowingly.

"You know, there are a lot of things in books," said the doll, "that are just made up. I didn't believe that story at all."

And that was very strange, because the story was … this one!

The Wind Who Went Away

Once upon a time, there was a fierce and fearsome wind who blew all day long around the little village of Belton.

The good people of Belton got together to decide what to do.

"We could build another windmill to use up the wind," suggested one man, but the miller objected that his business would be halved.

"We could stay indoors," suggested an old lady who didn't get out much anyway.

"We could pay the wind to go away," suggested the bank manager.

In the end, no one could agree about what to do, so the people went home to their houses, blown and buffeted all the way.

Now, the wily old wind had been listening. He decided he would teach the villagers a lesson. There and then, he packed his bags and went off to the mountains.

The next day, everything was still. For a few hours, everyone was very happy. Then the complaints began.

"I can't fly my kite!" cried the miller's son.

"My laundry won't get dry!" groaned the greengrocer.

"The sailing ship bringing my goods from China is stuck out in the bay," said a merchant.

I wish I could say that the people of Belton are more careful about complaining now, but they're not. The other day, I heard them moaning that the summer was too hot. I'm very much afraid the sun heard them too.

Look Out!

One morning, when Joshua Jones was reading his biggest book of fairytales, he fell in! He found he was sitting in the middle of a road with a little pig peering down at him.

"Get up! Get up!" cried the pig. "The wicked old wolf is right behind us, and we must get to my house before he comes."

But when Joshua saw the pig's little house, he stopped.

"Come on!" cried the pig.

Joshua Jones shook his head. "I've read this story," he said. "Your house is made of straw, and the wolf will huff and puff and blow it down."

"Then we must run on to my brother's house," said the little pig.

314

But when Joshua saw the little pig's brother's house, he shook his head again.

"This house is made of sticks," he said. "The wolf will huff and puff and blow it down. Trust me."

Five minutes later, Joshua Jones, the little pig, and the little pig's brother arrived at a brick house.

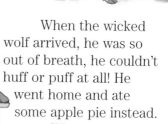

When the wicked wolf arrived, he was so out of breath, he couldn't huff or puff at all! He went home and ate some apple pie instead.

What happened to Joshua Jones? Well, as there was no fire in the grate, he climbed up the chimney and out of the book—just in time for his own supper.

Clarissa Cow

One day, George, who looked after the cows on White Fence Farm, brought his little niece to see them. Of course, one or two of them came across to say hello. as cows do, and one of these was Clarissa.

As soon as she saw the friendly cow, with the big black patch on her forehead, the little girl smiled. "Look!" she said, "it's the cow that jumped over the moon!" I expect you know the rhyme she was thinking of.

But Clarissa the cow did not know it. She listened as the little girl recited the whole poem. Then George took his niece off to the farmhouse and left Clarissa with a head full of silly ideas.

That very same day, Clarissa began jumping. *Thud! Thump! Lump! Thud!*

That night, Clarissa waited until the moon was big and full. She jumped and she jumped and she jumped, but there was no way she could even touch the moon, never mind jump over it. Clarissa felt sad as she walked slowly back to her barn.

But in the barnyard there was a puddle. And in the puddle … there was a moon! Clarissa couldn't believe it. She trotted as fast as she could … and jumped— right over the moon!

Of course, no one saw it. And no one would have believed it if they had been told. But from that day, Clarissa has walked as proudly as a queen, and everyone can see that.

The Precious Baby

Once upon a time there was a very precious baby. Everyone loved the baby. They tickled, and the baby giggled. They said *coo, coo, coo,* and the baby said *goo, goo, goo.* They rocked the baby, and the baby smiled. They swung the baby, and the baby laughed. They threw the baby up in the air, and the baby cried *oooooooh!* and came down safe and sound.

Each night the baby's chubby arms and legs splished and splashed in the bath. The bubbles winked, and the little ducks bobbed, and the baby giggled and squiggled. Then with a one, two, three, a big fluffy towel went all the way around the baby's slippery little body. There was squeezing and cuddling and bouncing … and bed.

There were so many cuddly toys in the baby's bed, there was hardly any room for the baby. Every night, there was snuggling and kissing, and someone who loved the baby very much said, "Goodnight, darling. Goodnight, sweetheart. See you in the morning!" And the baby smiled and went to sleep … almost every night. And in the middle of the night, sometimes the baby felt a butterfly kiss, light as love, on baby hair.

In the morning, the baby was the first one to wake up. The baby's bright little eyes looked all around. The baby's fat little feet bounced on the bed. The baby's little pink mouth opened wide and let everybody know it was time to get up.

And so it went on. Then one day the baby heard someone say, "Our baby isn't a baby any more. Our baby is growing up!" And the baby wrapped chubby little arms around the someone's knees and kissed them.

Do you know who that baby was? It was *you*! Goodnight, darling. Goodnight, sweetheart. Goodnight!